Do Butterflies Go To Heaven?

November Nichols

ISBN: 0692781803
ISBN 13: 9780692781807
Library of Congress Control Number: 2016915428
Papillon Press LLC, Decatur, GA

This book is dedicated to my one and only.
I see the best of me in you.
I love you in good times and bad times.

ACKNOWLEDGMENTS

To God, thank you for allowing me to be the vessel through which this story is told. I know you only put stories and experiences in people to allow them to be shared, so hopefully this helps someone through their journey to truth as much as it has helped me. As the old spiritual goes, I don't believe you brought me this far to leave me. So with that, here it goes:

To my spirit baby, darling boy and now grown man, thank you for choosing me as you floated around in the atmosphere looking for a mother to birth you. Thank you for loving me in spite of myself. When you entered my world, you changed my life for the better. Mommy will always love you. For you, I am forever grateful.

To my family, friends, and NNF's, sometimes life ain't pretty; thank you for loving me through it in the best way you know how. To Kenya and Monica for your constant encouragement, perspectives, and for reading my drafts. To my editors Mickey Platko and Carrie Weniger, thank you for helping me to accomplish a dream and for helping me to bring this story to life. For you all, I am forever grateful.

To Kenny, Dre, and Nicole for the invitation, and for feeding my spirit and helping me to see myself clearly once again, flaws and all. I started writing this book over twenty years ago, and began again as we sailed. I doubt it would have ever been completed without our journey together. To you three, I say, "You don't know what you don't know until you know." I am forever grateful.

To ALL, you know who you are, thank you for allowing me to be my authentic self and loving me in the most perfect way. You encouraged me to be brave and to tell my story, even when I was afraid and wanted to hide. For that, I am forever grateful.

To the one who said this book was trash. Maybe it is, but it's my trash and I own it. Thank you for teaching me to love myself more. To you, I am forever grateful.

To all of the butterflies that are still caterpillars and those who are still in their cocoons fighting to live life on their terms, be still and allow it. To those who, through their own struggles, have been beautifully transformed and dare to live their dreams boldly, God willing, and through divine grace, we will all make it to heaven. Thank you for allowing me to share...to live and dream in color. To God, I am forever grateful.

MAY 11, 1997

The evening she walked into my life was one I will never forget. It's funny how a single moment or event can change life as you know it forever.

We celebrated my very first Mother's Day at Pano's and Paul's, an exclusive restaurant in Atlanta. Pano's and Paul's is one of my favorite restaurants, and we go there for special occasions—anniversaries, birthdays, you know, shit like that. Only Mr. Pano evokes all of your senses in such a perfect way. The plush red velvet sofas, finely dressed servers, elegant food, and music all contributed to the luxurious mood.

Christian and I had just finished discussing the possibility of him working for my father when the maître d' approached our table.

"Sir, are you expecting any additional guests? There is a guest in the lobby who says she is your sister."

"She must be mistaken. I have no sister," Christian responded.

The maître d' nodded and walked away. We continued our conversation as we enjoyed our stuffed prawns drizzled with beurre blanc. A couple of minutes later, just as we were getting back into our groove, the maître d' returned.

"Pardon me again, sir. The lady insists that she is your sister, and that she needs to speak with you now."

"Look, I don't have a sister. I don't know who that is out there but they are obviously confused," Christian replied.

"Christian, you haven't even gone out there yet. Maybe it's Heidi," I said. We had just gotten off the phone with my sister-in-law and she'd said they were in the area. "Maybe they decided to stop by, or it could be someone you went to school with who spotted us on the way in."

Christian's handsome, caramel face crinkled and his brow furrowed. His light brown eyes squinted at my speculations. It was clear that he had no intention of going out to the lobby to see who was there.

"Look, I'll just go out there to see who it is because obviously she isn't going to leave until you acknowledge her," I said.

"Kami, we're enjoying our meal, let the restaurant handle that," Christian said while attempting to grab my arm before I marched off to the elegantly dressed lobby.

I had no idea that shit was about to hit the fan.

As I rounded the corner I spotted a woman sitting in an opulent velvet and brocade high-back chair. She was the only person in the lobby that looked nervous and out of place wearing skintight black stonewashed jeans and heels. I could see she was long-legged, probably taller than I am, which isn't difficult since I stand at all of five feet, two inches on a good day, five feet, six inches with heels on.

Long, wavy, coal black hair cascaded down her back and danced around her exotic facial features. *Where was she from?*

I asked myself as I glanced in the mirror to check my makeup and my short blonde pixie-cut hair. She looked like she was from another country.

With a smile I walked over to her and said, "Hello, I'm Kameleon. Are you looking for Christian?"

Frowning, she looked at me, rolled her eyes, and replied coldly with a heavy South African accent, "Yes, I am."

Attempting to be cordial despite her rudeness, I said, "Well, why don't you come in and join us?"

After glancing at the door, the woman silently stood and followed me as I walked toward the dining room.

Smiling at her again I asked, "Do you live in the area? How do you know Christian? Did you two go to school together?"

The woman remained stone-faced and silent.

Her silence made me a bit uneasy but after numerous attempts to strike up a conversation and no response, I led her back to the table in silence. *To hell with her* I thought giving no additional attention as to who she was or what she might want.

To be honest, I didn't care; all I was thinking about was the fried lobster tail that was waiting on me back at the table.

As we turned the corner to enter the dining room, Christian looked up at us with terror in his eyes, mouth hanging open in disbelief as we walked toward him. His face froze, so stoic that you would have thought he had gazed into Medusa's eyes and been transformed into stone.

The woman sat down next to me, sandwiching me in between her and Christian, and said "Hello, Christian."

Our elegant and intimate booth had all of a sudden become too small. Trying to create some personal space between the woman and me, I scooted closer to Christian and collected the tail of my dress. Her wide hips were plastered on it.

"Hello." he replied, His voice scratchy and thin.

She then turned to look at me and asked in a low, deliberate tone, "Are you his date?"

Who was this woman? Why did she feel empowered to ask me anything, especially when she had refused to answer any of my questions? *Rude bitch.*

"No" I said, "I'm his wife."

"Oh." She said. Her eyebrows went up. "Really now?"

"Yes, and now who are you?" I asked, not really sure if I wanted to know the answer. Suddenly, frightened of what I might hear, I shook my legs under the table in nervous anticipation of her response.

"I'm Wynter, Christian's girlfriend. We've been together a year and a half. I thought the two of you were separated. Christian said you were getting a divorce."

"He did, did he?" I said softly as I cut my eyes at Christian and then looked back at the woman that was now seated at our table. *I invited her there!*

My face was blood red and my stomach was somewhere near my fuckin' throat. I turned to face my husband, who looked like he was trying to make himself disappear but had forgotten his magic wand at home.

"Christian, is she your girlfriend? Really? When were you planning on letting me know that we were getting a divorce?"

"Kami, I..." Christian stuttered trying to find words.

Wynter finally smiled, as if pleased with herself. Then, she interrupted Christian and began to lay out his plan to leave me in excruciating detail, explaining how they planned to raise our son Ethan together.

As she talked, my heart sank, my face burned, and I could feel the blood pounding through my veins. I had heard enough.

Through clenched teeth I said, "Wynter, the divorce part is easy to arrange." I brought my head up to face her. "You, however, have cracked your fucking head wide open if you think I am going to allow you and this crooked ass nigga sitting next to me to raise my child."

By that time, Christian was a moot point—but believe you me, I felt like slapping the shit out of both of them when I heard my child's name come out of Wynter's mouth. *Was that crazy bitch on drugs or what?*

I noticed the servers were moving toward us at a feverish pace to try to extinguish the emotional fire that had ignited at our table.

As if realizing she had wreaked enough havoc on my evening, Wynter slowly stood up and without a glance backward, walked out.

What happened next almost set my ass over the top. Christian, the same motherfucker who had been speechless throughout her entire disclosure, got up and hurried after her.

If I had not been in such a nice establishment where the owners knew my family intimately, I would have shown the fuck out. Had he forgotten whom the fuck his wife was? Had he forgotten that we were supposed to be celebrating the fact that I had birthed his child less than a year ago? His only child? That this was my first Mother's Day? *My day?*

Apparently so, because he walked out right behind his bitch, leaving me sitting at the table with everyone in that fancy-ass restaurant looking at me. No one would look me in my eyes but I knew what they were thinking. "Why do they always have to bring their bullshit into our neighborhood instead of leaving it in the ghetto where they belong?"

I sighed, then tried to gather my faculties and wrap my head around what had just happened to me. Then, I walked my ass outside to find out what the hell was going on, because someone had some serious explaining to do. I wanted to hear whatever Christian had to say to her to make sure that there could be no lies coming from him later. He always had the amazing ability to twist details and words in his favor. In other words, he was a good ass liar (tiny detail everyone in his family had forgotten to share with me until after we were married).

By the time I got outside, Christian and Wynter were half-way down the sidewalk. I hurried in their direction, teetering off balance in my Gucci heels and trying not to bust my ass.

When Wynter saw me coming, she turned and rushed away.

Christian walked toward me, trying to explain.

I couldn't hear him. I still could not believe his ass had actually left me at the table to follow her. *I was his damn wife. What about me? Who was going to comfort me?*

"Shut the fuck up, Christian. Get my food packed and pay the fucking bill."

The magnitude of what had happened did not hit me until we were in the car. Overwhelmed with emotion, I began to cry uncontrollably.

What had he done? Why had he betrayed me like this? I was so confused. Through tears, I replayed the events of the evening, from Wynter's entrance through her exit. His betrayal rocked me like he had struck me with a hammer. How could I not know?

How could he live so comfortably in two different worlds?

I turned to my good-for-nothing low-down stank ass husband and said, "Take me to my parents' house."

At that moment, he reached over so as to touch me and said, "Honey, let me…"

Why do they always feel the need to touch you when they know that you're mad as hell? What could he possibly say to me? I raised my right hand and said in a frigid, ominous tone, "Don't you dare touch me."

Christian's eyes widened as he looked up at my hand. I glanced at it as well and noticed I was clutching the steak knife from dinner. Until that moment, I had not realized it was still in my hand and I'd carried it out with me.

JUNE 26, 1986

The blinds on the windows shook and rattled against the already cracked windowpanes as the wind howled outside with tornado force.

"We have to secure these windows," Grandma Delores shouted as she scurried from room to room, directing everyone to help prepare for what was to be the fourth hurricane to hit South Baton Rouge Parish in the last two months. It was gloomy and dark outside, foreshadowing the storm to come.

"Come on you girls, get up and help."

My sisters and I were terrified. We sat, still as statues, huddled together watching everyone around us prepare for what was familiar to them yet unfamiliar to us.

Storms of this kind rarely occurred in Atlanta where we lived. However, in Baton Rouge, Louisiana, this was the norm. It seemed like every time we visited my step-grandmother's house, torrential rains erupted. It was almost as if the weather was trying to warn us—mainly me—of what was to come. We didn't like visiting them because things were never peaceful.

They treated us differently—especially me. Something always happened.

Since my sisters and I spent the majority of our summer there each year instead of Atlanta, we had to endure dividing our time between both sides of the family. We visited Grandma Delores's only because we loved our Daddy so much, and we knew it would hurt his feelings if we did not spend time with *his people* too.

Our visits were solely out of obligation, and they were always rehearsed. We knew the drill—if we wanted to see our favorite toys again, we always had to leave them at Auntie Mina's house, and we always got the admonition, "Please be quiet, don't ask questions, and don't draw attention to yourselves, no matter what."

We knew better than to say it out loud, but as we peered at each other, our eyes said it all. At this moment more than ever, Dia, Lynie, and I would much rather be with our Auntie Mina or Grandma Belle. Instead, here we were, stuck at this damn house, in the middle of a hurricane, with no hope of returning to safety any time soon.

Grandma Delores was my sisters' biological grandmother. She and the rest of the family inherited me when my mother and stepfather decided to marry. I never thought of Daddy as my stepfather though, he had been raising me since I was three years old and had officially adopted me when I was eight. He was the only Daddy I had ever known. I will never forget the day I asked him, after Lynie was born "Daddy, why is my name different from everyone in the family?"

He said, "Baby, we can fix that." The next thing I knew, my last name was Papillon just like everyone else's.

"What'chy'all lookin' at? Ain't'chy'all never seen wind and rain before? Scared ass children."

Aunt Stevie's loud, slurred; drunken words were like Satan's song. We watched her intently as she stumbled about the room half-clothed from the evening before, head rag cocked to the side, partially covering her left eye. As drunk as she was, it was a wonder she had not fallen on her face. How could she be drunk at nine in the morning?

Dia and Lynie were too young to realize what they were looking at, but me, since I had been the only child for so long and had mainly been around adults, at the ripe age of twelve, I knew what was up with her sorry ass. For God's sake, we had just gotten out of bed and she reeked of alcohol and funk. Her smell was so pungent that my nose stung with each pass that she made across the room.

"Leave them children alone," Grandma Delores said with a nervous chuckle. "They are just not used to this kind of weather, that's all."

"We all runnin' 'round here helpin', and they just sittin' there like bumps on a log. Like they too damn pretty to help."

In a split second, just as Aunt Stevie muttered her last drunken word, darkness and quiet simultaneously covered the entire house. Until that point, I had managed to keep my sisters calm and quiet. But when the lights went out, all hell broke loose. Dia and Lynie immediately started screaming and crying.

"Aww shit. Now we have to listen to this crap for God knows how long," Aunt Stevie mumbled.

How dare that evil woman allow God's name to come from her filthy lips? I thought to myself as I sprang to my feet.

My stupid cousins Thomas and Tatum were always up to something. They were Stevie's children, but she left them for Grandma Delores to take care of as she gallivanted around Baton Rouge getting drunk and high off God knows what. Once, I had overheard my parents saying that they were concerned about Aunt Stevie milking Grandma Delores for cash to support her drug habit.

Aunt Stevie was Grandma Delores's only daughter and problem child. Tatum and Thomas were following in their mother's footsteps, proving themselves to be quite a handful. Tatum was eight and Thomas was five, like Dia, and their primary goal was to harass us girls to the point of tears. They knew Dia and Lynie were already scared, and that playing around with the lights would put them over the top, one step closer to accomplishing their goal of terrorizing us.

In hopes of restoring light and calm, I ran with all of my might to each light switch, clicking each one vigorously up and down and saying quietly, "Please come back on, please come back on."

Nothing happened.

I realized that it was not Tatum and Thomas fooling around—the power really was out. I ran to the window, and saw that the once heavy and now heavier winds outside had snapped the power line that was connected to the house. The loose line was flapping in the middle of the street like a cowboy's lasso, shooting firework-like sparks in all directions.

I stifled a scream.

I was the oldest in our family—"the big sister"—and I was charged with the responsibility of taking care of and protecting my little sisters. My Mama had told me that I was supposed to take care of them...but right then, I was scared too. A huge lightning bolt crackled across the sky, hitting the old oak tree that the swing hung from, causing ancient timbers to come crashing down, crushing both the fence and the abandoned car that was parked in the empty lot next to the house.

"Kami. Where are you, Kami?" my sisters screamed from the other room between sobs.

Remembering that I had left them in the room alone with that evil woman, I ran back and wrapped my twelve-year-old arms around them, hoping to comfort and quiet them. Their cries subsided, but the wind and rain did not. Heavy drops pounded the roof with such force that I thought it was going to give way at any moment.

My sisters and I sat close to the window, clinging to each other for dear life, praying that the rain would go away, and wishing that we could go home—home to Atlanta, or home to Auntie Mina's, where we were safe.

Littered paper and the sign from the corner store across the street were flying through the air. The stop light in front of the house that once directed drivers in the busy intersection was blinking uselessly. Not that there was any traffic to direct. No one was on the street. It was like a ghost town outside as large puddles began to form around the house, and all around the surrounding neighborhood.

"Come girls, move away from the window. Your sitting there staring at it isn't going to make it stop any faster," Grandma Delores said.

Delores was a kind woman, usually very focused on her appearance. A chocolate-brown lady with ebony eyes, who stood all of four foot eleven. Today, because she had nowhere special to go, she slopped around the house in a leopard print head scarf, a red and gold muumuu, and high-heeled slippers. However, when she went out, she was sharp as a tack.

She would always say, "A lady has to be the best, have the best, and, most of all, look her best at all times."

Grandma Delores was a schoolteacher by trade, and had taught at McKinley High School for twenty-five years. She was the sponsor of McKinley's infamous May Night, where many talented singers and actresses got their starts. Everyone knew Grandma Delores. She was one of the best-dressed women in South Baton Rouge. On any given Sunday, she would break out with one of her legendary outfits, which was comprised of a hat, a suit, and the most beautiful pair of stilettos you could ever imagine. To this day, I believe in my heart that she is one of the reasons for my clothing and accessory fetish. Last summer while I was playing in her closet, I counted over 200 pairs of shoes, and just as many (if not more) hats and handbags.

When Aunt Stevie wasn't using drugs and she and her kids were away, I liked playing in Grandma Delores's closet. However, Grandma Delores's closet room also doubled as the room that Aunt Stevie used when she got too high to be alone at her own house, or take care of herself and her badass children.

"Why don't you children play a game or something? That will make the time go by faster," Grandma Delores suggested.

"I'm scared. I don't want to play," Lynie was in her six-year-old cranky mode.

"What should we play?" Dia asked. She sniffled and tears dropped from her eyes, but even though her voice was squeaky and thin, she sounded a lot more cheerful than Lynie.

"We don't have any power, and I can't see in here," Lynie continued.

"What about Monopoly?" Grandma Delores suggested. "We have plenty of lanterns and candles in the house. Surely we can muster enough light for you all to be able to see the game board. What do you guys say?"

Before we could respond, Grandma Delores had spread a blanket on the floor of her guest bedroom where we slept the night before, found the game, and whipped up enough light to illuminate the entire bedroom.

Dia, Lynie, Thomas and Tatum settled into their first round of Monopoly. Grandma Delores moved to the kitchen to clean our breakfast dishes, and Aunt Stevie's loud drunken ass had passed out on the leather sofa in the study. Thank God she passed out before she made it to Grandma Delores's closet room. I could play with the shoes.

My sisters, Tatum and Thomas were so consumed with their game that they didn't even notice when I slipped out of the room. I walked to the kitchen where Grandma Delores was washing dishes and asked, "Grandma Delores, is it ok for me to play in your closet?"

She smiled gently and said, "Sure darling, just make sure you leave things the way you found them."

You would have thought that I had just won the lottery. With unbelievable excitement, I said, "Oh, thank you so much. I promise I will not tear anything up, I'll be super careful, and leave your closet as if I was never in there."

Grandma Delores smiled. She knew that I would cherish and take care of her things. That's why I was the only one who could play in that closet. I was always trustworthy and responsible, and always left her closet neater than it was before.

I grabbed one of the five lanterns that lined the hallway, and moved to what was certainly the best room in the entire house. The walls were painted a rich garnet red to accent the grand mahogany four-poster bed that deceivingly served as the focal point of the not-so-large room.

The bed linens were plush, crafted out of black and gold velvet brocade and trimmed with bullion fringe. Elaborate cream, black, and gold-striped shantung silk draperies covered the large picture frame windows and completed the room.

The room was straight out of a swank French magazine. An ornate silver full-length mirror in the last available corner in the room provided a frame for the many glorious fashions it reflected.

My mind raced and my heart pounded as I eagerly began to open the large mahogany double doors that secured Grandma Delores's couture. What new items had she added since my last visit? She always placed her new items in the section on the left. Would her shoes fit me this time? Last year, my shoe size had been five and a half and I flopped clumsily around the house trying to maintain my balance. Now I was a size six and a half. The same shoe size she was. I could not wait to see what was behind the mahogany doors. Just as I lifted the first Gucci box, a scream came from the guest bedroom—the room where my sisters, Tatum and Thomas were playing Monopoly.

"Shit." I softly placed the box on the floor and moved toward the door to see what was going on.

Dia met me in the doorway of Grandma Delores's closet room with tears in her eyes.

"What's wrong, Dia?" I was hoping to quiet her before she woke up Cruella Deville.

"My money is gone," she said.

"What do you mean, your money is gone?" I replied.

"It's gone, Kami." Her voice grew louder and shriller. "I showed it to Thomas yesterday and then put it back in my purse. Today, when I went to show them again while we were playing, it was gone."

"Why were you showing your money off?" I said. "You know better than that."

"They said I didn't have any, and I told them I did, and that Mama and Daddy never sent us anywhere without money."

"Dia, I told you to keep your money hidden and not to show off. This is what happens when you show off."

Dia sobbed.

"Stop crying," I said. "Let's go ask the boys if they know what happened to it."

I knew who took it. Thomas was always doing things to Dia to hurt her. I knew his ass had it. As we entered the room, I could tell that he was guilty.

He was fidgeting and refused to look me in the eye.

"Have you seen Dia's money, Thomas?"

"Naw, I haven't seen it. Maybe she spent it and didn't remember."

"Thomas, you and I both know we didn't go anywhere to spend any money. We just got here yesterday, and today we are in the middle of a damn hurricane. Where could she have gone to spend money?"

"Uh...uh, I don't know, all I know is that I don't have it."

"Ok, if you don't have it, empty your pockets and your secret drawer."

"I ain't doin' nothing. I told you I don't have it."

"Ok fine, then I'm going to go tell Grandma Delores."

"Fine, go tattle."

I grabbed Dia and Lynie by the hands and stormed to the kitchen where Grandma Delores was cleaning.

"Grandma Delores, Dia had one hundred dollars in her purse that Mama and Daddy gave her. Yesterday, she showed Thomas her money, and today it's gone. He's the only person in the house that knew she had that money except for me and Lynie, and we have our own money. Will you please ask Thomas to empty his pockets and his secret drawer?"

"Kami, are you sure that Dia didn't forget it at your Auntie Mina's?"

"If she left it, how could she have shown it to Thomas?"

"And Thomas said he saw it?" she asked

"Yes."

"Thomas. Thomas," Grandma Delores screamed. She motioned to us and stomped out of the kitchen.

Before we even got out the door with Grandma Delores, Aunt Stevie was already cussing her way up the hall.

She pointed at me. "How dare your little ass accuse my child of stealin'? Y'all ain't got nuthin' to steal."

"Aunt Stevie, Dia showed Thomas her money yesterday, and today it is gone." I could hear my voice shake, confronting her anger.

"My child ain't no thief."

"Well then if he isn't, why wouldn't he show me his pockets and his secret drawer?"

"How dare you talk to me like that you little bitch. You always were a little troublemaker. I knew that from the moment I laid eyes on yo' little ass. You think you know everything. Too grown for yo' own damn good. Bring yo' ass here. I'm gonna beat yo' little ass for lyin' on my son."

"I'm not coming to you."

"Oh yes, you will."

Aunt Stevie grabbed my arm and tore at my clothes.

"You need a good ass whippin'. That'll set you straight."

My sisters shrieked. "No, no, stop,"

I heard them behind me.

"Aunt Stevie, no," Dia screamed.

I didn't hear a single word from Grandma Delores, who stood paralyzed with her fucking mouth open.

Thomas's slimy ass had slithered out of sight in the commotion.

I struggled to get loose from Aunt Stevie, and finally broke her hold. I leaned down to grab my sisters' hands. As I stood, my mouth met the palm of Aunt Stevie's hand.

I felt a stinging sensation above my lip and tasted blood in my mouth.

"Bitch."

I rose up and, out of nowhere, with all the might in my small body I punched her in the jaw.

She fell back on the grand mahogany bed in the opulent closet room.

I grabbed my sister's hands and we ran.

From behind, Aunt Stevie leapt up and grabbed for me, missing me by a hair as I pulled my sisters through the hallway at the speed of light. We ran right into Grandpa Papillon, who had come home in all the commotion.

I stopped, looked up at him, and saw the expression on his face. He was staring over my shoulder, his eyes tight.

I looked back.

Aunt Stevie had stopped dead in her tracks. She was looking back at him, her mouth hanging open.

He grabbed me up in his big strong arms and said, "What happened to your mouth, darling?"

"Aunt Stevie slapped me."

"Why?" he asked as he cut his eyes at her.

"I don't know, ask her."

"Well Stevie, why did you slap her?"

"Well, I...ur...I...she lied on Thomas?"

"Did she? What did she say?"

"She said that he stole Dia's money, and my child ain't no thief."

"Did you say that Thomas took Dia's money, Kami?"

"Yes."

"Why?"

"Dia showed Thomas the money that Mama and Daddy gave her for the trip yesterday, and today it's gone."

"What makes you so certain he has it?"

"I asked him to empty his pockets and his secret drawer, and he wouldn't."

"How do you know that he didn't take the money, Stevie?"

"My child ain't no thief, he don't steal. Dia know she lost that money."

"Where is Thomas? I think it is very odd that he is no-where around to defend himself. Thomas. Thomas," Grandpa called.

"Yes, Grandpa."

"Come here."

Thomas slowly moved close to Grandpa.

"I am going to ask you this one time. Did you take Dia's money?"

"No Grandpa."

"Are you sure?"

"Yes, I'm sure."

"Ok, then empty your pockets and open that drawer."

Everyone's eyes were focused on Thomas. This was the moment of truth.

He slowly emptied the contents of his front pockets, and then the back ones. There was no money. He turned toward the drawer, and I could see his eyes as he fumbled with the combination. He looked scared.

Grandpa gently placed me on the ground and moved closer to Thomas.

"Boy, you better open that drawer right now."

No sooner did the words fall from Grandpa's lips then the drawer opened and out fell Dia's money.

Grandpa Papillon grabbed Thomas by the neck and whipped his belt off all in one motion.

Everyone stood, looking at the money on the floor.

I knew he had taken the money.

I turned and started packing my bags. I would call Grandma Belle and Papa to come get me.

Come hell or high water, nothing could make me stay in that house another moment. Even if I had to walk through the hurricane all the way to 4240 Wells Street, nothing could keep me there.

That day, Aunt Stevie taught me a very painful truth. I carried the name Papillon, but no matter how badly I wanted to be a part, *to some*, I would never have a true place in this family. I was different and regardless of how much Daddy loved and accepted me, he was my *stepfather* in their eyes.

Through tears over the phone, I told Grandma Belle and Papa what had happened, and before I knew it they were standing at the edge of the high water in front of the Papillon's driveway, their faces grim and angry. They didn't look surprised. They looked prepared. Prepared to comfort me, to love me, to protect me, to take me home. They were my life preservers—my family.

I brushed tears from my eyes as I gathered my sisters and listened to the muted angry words of the adults.

Finally, Grandma and Papa walked up to us, took our things, and we left.

As I walked out the front door, somehow, I knew it was a turning point, and that things would be different. I knew that was my last sleepover visit at the Papillon's and my heart hurt when I realized that I had made my last visit to my beloved closet room.

I sat, silent, in the backseat of the car as Papa drove us to their house across town. My sisters napped, but I watched Papa as he drove.

Frequently, he looked back at me.

His eyes looked sad. I could tell that he was hurting because I was hurting. That he wanted to make the pain go away—to completely erase the experience from my mind.

"Baby, how are you doing back there?"

"I'm okay, Papa."

"What Aunt Stevie did was wrong, child. Nobody deserves to get hit like that."

I turned to the side window to hide my tears. What did I do wrong? I was protecting my sister.

"We'll talk about this later, okay?"

My heart throbbed with the realization that I would never forget what happened today. Never ever. And I think Papa knew that.

I tried to smile at him, but it hurt. All I could muster was a slight curve on one side of my mouth. My legs were moist from the rain. I had to keep adjusting to keep them from sticking to the plastic on the back seat of the Chevy Nova.

My grandma saw me shuffling around and said, "We're almost home honey—just hold on."

Until that moment at the Papillon's, I had never felt different. I knew my name had been different. I knew I had a different biological father than my sisters. I knew my mother had been married before and that I was the product of that marriage, but I was never treated differently. In our home Daddy never made me feel that there was a difference between my sisters and me. Now, however, I wondered if I was being *tolerated* by the rest of the Papillon family.

I was too young to remember why my Mama left my biological father. No one ever took the time to explain it. My Mama, Avery, met my *real* father, Jordan, while visiting her sister Lynn at the University of Southern Louisiana, and the relationship was fast and furious.

"Before we knew it, you were here," my Mama told me once, with a smile on her face.

I was two years old when we left my father. When I grew old enough to ask about him, Mama told me that my dad didn't know how to handle the pressures of being a father and husband, and it was best that we went with Papa and Grandma Belle to allow him time to get his life together.

What pressure? Why couldn't we all stay together? I had never fully understood, and it had been a while since I even thought about it.

Mama was the youngest of Papa's five children, and I was his first grandchild.

Papa said, "Hell would have had to freeze over two times before I allow anyone to hurt or neglect you and your mom."

All I know is that things must have been pretty damn bad if Papa drove from Baton Rouge to Lafayette on a weeknight to get us. Baton Rouge Parish is really only about fifty miles away from Lafayette—however on the day we left, it spoke volumes that Papa was already around the corner from our apartment and it was only five P.M. That meant he had worked his seven thirty to three thirty shift all day in the hot sun for Mr. Hershey, and had not yet been home to eat the cabbage and cornbread that my Grandma Belle prepared for him every night for supper.

Papa was always coming to my rescue. The first time was when he came to get Mama and me from my Dad in Lafayette and now he was rescuing me in the middle of a hurricane from my *step-Daddy's* people's house.

My thoughts were interrupted by Papa's announcement. "We're here, Kami. You and the girls run inside with Grandma and I'll get your things."

Once inside, Grandma helped us to get settled and ran me a hot bath. Their home was comfortable, and smelled like the cabbage and cornbread Grandma had been cooking before they ran out to get me.

I sat quietly on the edge of the bed as Grandma bustled about looking for some ointment for my lip. She then sat down next to me and cradled my face in her hands. She gently pushed my curls out of my face and said, "Let me have a look at that cut."

As soon as she touched me, all of my emotions came charging back like a stampede of wild horses. I began to cry uncontrollably, releasing all of the hurt, fear, and anger I was holding in my little body. I held onto her as if my life depended on it. I could not pull myself together, and she could not pry me off of her—nor did she try. She held onto me as tightly as I was holding onto her, apologizing for my pain through her embrace.

"Now now, my darling child," she said. "Everything is going to be just fine. Papa and I are here, and you're safe. You never have to go there again unless you want to. Let it go, my love. Just try to let it go."

MAY 11, 1997

I remember the tired, solemn look in my mother's blood-shot eyes the day she left my father. She looked like she hadn't slept in days, eyes couched in fear while inwardly, she roared with anger about the deep, life-changing secret that had been revealed to her.

I remember kissing her and trying to wiggle my way onto her lap just to be close to her. I knew she was hurting. I could feel her pain in my little body. That's the connection between mother and child that people describe.

For a fleeting moment, I wished my son Ethan was here right now—to kiss me and wiggle his way onto my lap to help me through this. Despite what my parents told me about the day we left my father, my mother's expression told me every-thing I needed to know. It told me that things would never be the same again. And, sitting in this car right now with this man, my husband, I know that things will never be the same for Christian and me.

This shit is surreal. I have lived through this pain before, only I was two and it was my mother who was suffering. Is this hereditary? Is this déjà vu? Is the same scene from my mother's life playing out in my own?

As we pulled into the driveway of my parent's home, my breath tightened again and my heart resumed its race. Never had I felt more connected to my mother. Our relationship has always been hot and cold because I have always quietly blamed her for me not knowing my father. In this single moment however, I was clear and at one with the pain that was in her eyes and heart the day Granddaddy came to get us.

"Kami, I never meant for this to happen. I never meant to hurt you like this," Christian said.

"You have been cheating on me since we got married, Christian," I screamed. "What did you think would happen? Did you think you wouldn't get caught? Did you think I'd never find out?"

I snorted and sniffled my tears as I stumbled my way out of the car. I didn't know whether I was angrier with him for cheating or her for not waiting until after my dinner to break the news to me. I was famished, humiliated, and pissed the fuck off all at the same time, and I could smell my fried lobster tail, which had been hurriedly wrapped in aluminum foil and shaped into a swan. I always loved the restaurant's attention to detail, a skill I often lacked when it came to matters of the heart. Lately I had been so consumed with school and my career. Maybe if I'd focused less on work and paid more attention to Christian, asked more questions, perhaps this wouldn't be happening.

Christian opened the back door for me.

My whole family was posted up at the kitchen island when we entered. When they noticed my expression, they turned and looked at Christian like, "Nigga what? Why does she look like that? You have some serious explaining to do."

"Kami, are you alright?" Mama asked noticing the redness in my eyes as we walked into the house. "You look like you've been crying honey, what's wrong?

When I didn't respond, Mama screamed, "For God's sake Christian, what's going on?"

"A situation happened at the restaurant. A woman I have been dating showed up."

"Dating. You bastard." Mama shrieked. "Who the hell are you dating besides your wife, Christian?"

"What do you mean showed up?" Daddy said.

Mama quickly moved towards me with Lynie and Dia close behind. She took the lobster I had been clutching like a life preserver out of my hands and handed it to Lynie to put in the refrigerator. "Come on honey," Mama said as she, Lynie and Dia wrapped their arms around me and ushered me to my parents' bedroom.

My dad stayed with Christian giving him the side eye, but it wasn't five minutes later when Daddy stuck his head in the room. "Christian and I are going to run out for a minute."

We all knew what that meant. Daddy was about to grill Christian.

As soon as they were gone, I recounted the entire awful story to my mother and sisters, while sobbing throughout. When I got to the part where Wynter told me about her and Christian's plans to raise Ethan, I choked up. I couldn't find my words. Lynie hugged my neck tightly giving me the strength to go on and finish the story.

By the time I was done, my father and my sorry ass husband walked in the door. I still don't know what my dad said to him, but whatever it was, it must have brought tears to Christian's eyes because they were red as hell and he was apologizing like a fool.

"Kami, I am so sorry. I love you and Ethan so much. I don't want to lose my family. I was wrong, baby, for cheating. I was just as surprised as you to see her at the restaurant and I don't know how she found out where we were. I know you can't imagine forgiving me for this right now baby but, please try. Please try to forgive me. Don't give up on me. Don't give up on our marriage and us."

After a few minutes, I got tired of his groveling, pathetic apologies.

If he'd been true to our vows, there'd be no need for apologies. He wouldn't have to beg to keep his family.

I was torn and struggled to decide whether I was going to stay with my parents for the night or return to my own house. I wanted to snuggle down in the comfort of my parents' home, my sisters surrounding me like a cocoon.

I remembered that I had left my friend Shani to babysit Ethan. Shani and I had become really good friends while teaching at Briarwood High School. We spent a lot of time together both in and out of school.

Although we were close, it would be too humiliating to explain why I didn't return to the house that evening, and I knew she would have millions of questions for me.

I sighed, then hugged my mom. "I've got to go Mama."

"Kami, please stay for at least one night. Separation will do you and Christian good." Mama said.

"I've got to go. I can't leave Ethan for the night. You know he would trip the fuck out without me there when he wakes."

Shani was spending the night with us, and I was not ready for anyone else to know my sordid story, so I had to make sure that everything remained as cheerful as it had been when I left earlier that evening. That meant I had to sleep in the same bed as my bastard of a husband. I can't describe how sick that made me.

The next morning, when I went into the guest room to iron my clothes for work, Shani smiled and asked, "How was last night, girl?"

"Fuck last night."

"Uh, you want to explain that comment?"

"No. Just let it be."

I fumbled around the room, pulling together my clothing for the day and setting up the ironing board. I could feel Shani's gaze on the back of my neck.

I'm sure she was stunned by my reply and wanted to ask so many more questions, but she just collected herself and said, "I'm here if you want to talk."

"Thanks," I managed to mumble and retreated to the bathroom before my eyes filled with tears. What was I to say?

My stomach turned as I remembered sitting sandwiched between Christian and his girlfriend. How long had this shit really been going on, and better yet, why? My mind churned with a million thoughts and questions. What had I missed? How did I not know this was happening? How did she know Ethan? Had she met him? How? When?

Anger flashed inside of me with that thought. Had Wynter been with my child? Had she? When I looked up, I realized that Christian had quietly, slowly, and cautiously entered the bathroom and stood in the doorway.

I turned away. The sight of him repulsed me. How could he betray me like this? How could he ruin our relationship? I had known him all my life, since I was six years old and he was seven, almost as long as he had known himself.

We had attended each other's birthday parties and gone on church retreats together.

He had been president of the teen club at our church, and I'd been vice president.

My thoughts were interrupted by Ethan's cry. Going to see about Ethan was just the diversion I needed to get out of that bathroom with Christian.

"I'll get him." Shani yelled from the other room.

"Dammit," I thought. Shani beat me to the punch. This left me no choice but to deal with Christian. I looked up at him with daggers in my eyes and moved close to him- so close, that he could feel my breath. I said through clenched teeth, "I was with you before you had anything. I helped you to build everything you have and this is how you repay me?"

Christian didn't dare move or comment. He was as still as stone with only his eyes darting around as if looking for an escape from the bathroom, which suddenly felt as if it had no windows and no doors.

"Does the life we have built and our history together count for anything?"

"Kami, it does," Christian whispered using what seemed to be his last breath.

I could no longer tell what was true and what wasn't. What was real and what wasn't. Was the love that we had shared real, true, and unmitigated?

"Why did you bring her into our lives, Christian? If honoring your vows was not your intent, then why did you marry me? I didn't ask you to marry me. You asked me. Why did you do that if you were not ready to be committed to our family and me? How could you be so evil and deceitful?"

Christian's head hung down facing the bathroom floor and his shoulders slouched in shame and defeat. He had been living two lives for over a year, and I had no clue.

"Answer me Christian. Was it because of school and the limited time I had outside of my studies? What made you do this to us?"

"I didn't feel needed" Christian managed to get out. "You're so strong. So ambitious. I didn't feel like you needed or wanted me."

"That's bullshit Christian," I said. "If you felt that way, why didn't you say anything? Don't you dare try to deflect your behavior onto me. You did this. You made this choice to go outside of our marriage."

I had to admit, I had been pouring every last minute into finishing my Master's program, and I was almost there. But I was constantly checking in with Christian, asking him how he was doing. How he was holding up through the process.

He always told me he was fine. This was the first mention of him having an issue, and I was damn near done. Now I know why he was fine. Here I was, trying to better myself and position myself for the next chapter of my life as an educator; trying to ensure that I could make a positive contribution to our family and our dreams. Meanwhile, my husband had obviously been doing the same, except his next chapter included Wynter instead of me.

I turned toward the mirror and looked at our reflections, allowing his response to sink in. We looked a mess.

I splashed water on my face, fixed myself as best I could, and walked up front to take Ethan from Shani.

"Thanks for everything. Sorry I was so grouchy this morning." I busied myself, fussing with the baby. "I know we had planned to ride to school together this morning, but I'm running so much later than I had anticipated and I don't want to make you late."

Shani smiled. "I completely understand. I overheard part of your conversation with Christian. Are you ok?" Shani asked.

I brushed her concern off with a thin smile. "I'm fine girl. Why don't you go ahead to school and I'll be right behind you. Promise."

"Okay," Shani replied as she was walking out the door. "Even though Christian's taking Ethan to daycare, I'll just tell Mr. Perry you had to drop Ethan at daycare and that you're on your way. That'll buy you some time to pull it together before you have to face your students."

That made me tear up a little. "Thank you so much Shani. I really appreciate you." Balancing Ethan on my hip, who was playing in my hair, I gave her a hug and closed the door behind her.

Christian had just entered the kitchen and was beginning to make coffee. Without a word, I kissed Ethan on the cheek and handed him to Christian so that they could get on with their morning routine and I headed to my bedroom to get dressed for work.

As I drove to school, I thought; everything I had been so sure of yesterday was now so uncertain. My entire marriage was a lie. My relationship with my husband was a complete calamity. My life was in shambles.

The previous night had rocked my belief system and changed my view of life and relationships. I was lost and hardened, and my trust was completely broken. I was changed forever, and now had to try to rebuild from the ground up.

But where to begin? God give me strength.

JUNE 8, 1997

Lord knows I love her.

Bless her heart. I know she didn't mean anything by it. I mean, that sweet little woman could not have possibly known that her dear, sweet baby boy would fuck up like this. Could she? As a child, I would sit in church and watch her. I didn't understand how she always looked so peaceful, deep in prayer like no one else had God's attention but her.

Velma Beck, Christian's mother, was a pretty, petite little lady with reddish-brown hair, a drop-dead gorgeous husband named Louis, and two handsome sons, Christian, and his older brother Braxton.

"Kami, stop staring at her," my mother would whisper on many occasions when I would forget the good manners that I had been taught and simply gawk at her and her attractive family.

Velma was one of the many Sunday school teachers at Saint Anthony's Catholic Church in Atlanta, Georgia. However, her class was the one that all of the girls would fight to be in, hoping that they would get an opportunity to hear stories about the things that her family had been doing or were going to do in the future.

We would listen to the stories about family trips to the mountains and the funny things that the boys had done during their vacations, not only because they were interesting, but mostly to find out where or how we could stumble upon the boys at their numerous sporting events. The girls all wanted an opportunity to get to know her sons a little better and the majority of them thought that the best way to do this was to get close to Mama first.

You know how the saying goes: "Get to the Mama and decrease the drama."

I really got what I asked for, I told myself. Now I'm a prisoner in my own house, in a broken marriage, trying to figure things out for Ethan's sake.

I know my little son senses the tension between his father and me. He is barely one, but how could he not? Things have been so awkward around the house since the horrible night at Pano's and Paul's that I can barely look at Christian. We have not slept in the same bed for the past month. Prior to the grand reveal, our Saturday mornings would consist of me cooking a huge breakfast, and afterward we would all pile up in the bed for family time and a mid-morning nap. The thought of that type of proximity this Saturday morning— and the potential of Christian's toes even grazing me—made me gag.

A few Saturdays ago, Ethan had begun to strategically crawl and position himself in between the guest bedroom where his father had been sleeping and the master bedroom where I slept so that he could see both of us and we could see him. When one of us went to get him, he would cry. When we put him back down, he would crawl back into position and just sit there looking back and forth between Christian and I. This Saturday was no different. I assume moving him prevented him from seeing one of us. I'm sure he wanted everything to be the same as it had been before. He didn't understand what had caused the divide.

Hell, I didn't understand.

Only Christian can explain, and I'm not talking to his ass right now. Nothing he could say could make me understand why he did this to us.

Everything that's happening to our little family is sad, I concluded. As I lay in bed, I thought about the past few weeks and how we couldn't agree on anything. Every conversation had turned into an argument. Where did all the love go so quickly? Oh yeah, I know: out the door with Wynter. I remembered the groveling Christian did at my parent's house, and how pathetic he looked.

What exactly is he sorry about? He wasn't sorry when he met her. He wasn't sorry when he was with her. He wasn't sorry when he took our son around her. He's only sorry because I know his secret and he doesn't know what I'm going to do. He doesn't know my angle.

My thoughts were interrupted by Ethan trying to sing some song. I got out of the bed, moved closer to him, smiled, and asked, "Honey, what are you trying to sing? Who taught you that?"

In his broken baby talk, Ethan managed to get out, "Shuck a rena."

Christian bolted from the guest bedroom headed toward Ethan and I so fast it looked like he was trying to prevent peeing his pants. His goal was to distract Ethan and get him to stop singing. Noticing the anxiety in Christian's eyes, I knew it could only be on thing. The song Ethan was singing must have been a song that Wynter had taught him. Ethan, not knowing any better was simply being silly, singing as he always did. Little did he know that one little word caused World War III to break out in our home.

"You let that bitch be with my son? Got him coming home singing songs to me that she taught him?" I was gasping in pain. "Really Christian? You're the scum of the earth. How could you do this? You have to know this is wrong. Have you no conscience?"

"Kami I'm sorry. He was only around her one time," Christian responded. "I had no idea he would remember the song and come home singing it. He's only ten months old."

"Ethan loves music and loves to sing. He's a sponge Christian. He'll remember that song just like he remembers Wynter. How could you?" I stomped back into my bedroom. Christian followed close behind me leaving Ethan, still singing, on the floor in the hallway in his spot.

"Kami, we can't go on like this forever. What are we going to do?" Christian's voice was soft. "I know you hate me and I deserve that, but I'm worried about you. You haven't eaten in days and you walk around here barely talking or saying anything. When I talk to you, you just look at me with this blank hollow stare. Talk to me please." He put his hand out, palm up. "I can't undo the past. I can only apologize, continue to ask for your forgiveness, and try to be a better man in the future."

For the last few weeks I have been remarkably quiet, reflective, and sullen, something that Christian is not accustomed to. Hell, this feeling is foreign to me too. Normally I'm bubbly, happy, ranting, raving, cussing, and fussing. But now, I just don't have it in me.

"Look Christian, I'm tired and weak. This Wynter situation has taken everything out of me. I don't feel like myself. I can't tell you what we're going to do or what's going to happen to us because I don't know. It takes everything in my power just to get out of bed and make it through my workday without failing to pieces. The pain has been consistent and consuming since the incident. I haven't felt this kind of betrayal since childhood. I am broken and grasping for ways to put the pieces of my heart and life back together."

"I understand Kami," Christian said. "Take all the time you need. I won't rush you, just please don't shut me out. Please don't give up on us." Christian turned and left.

Ethan was now lying on his back giggling and playing with his feet. I watched Christian as he reached to scoop Ethan up off the floor.

I turned back to look out the window and thought, *Can I put the pieces back together? Can we put the pieces back together?*

Christian had opened Pandora's Box.

The night after the incident, my mother finally revealed that she'd left my father because he was a drug-abusing womanizer who brought venereal diseases home to her.

She said, "I had a baby daughter to raise. I couldn't continue to risk my health by staying with him. I was only nineteen, but I had to get out of that situation. "

Listening to my mother I realized, I really could have become a statistic, judging from the direction Jordan Sanford Dean was going at that time.

Why had she waited so long to share?

More memories from childhood began to consume me. Growing up, I always wanted to be perfect. Mistakes and failures were not an option for me—not for Kami Papillon. Although I made many, we always found a way to overcome them or cover them up.

As a young mother with little education, my Mama struggled to make ends meet until she met my step-father, whom I adore with every ounce of me. He changed our lives and helped me to realize that I was capable of being loved and achieving anything my heart desired. He and my Mama wanted more for my sisters and me than they had.

I grew up not wanting to end up like my Mama, sacrificing my dreams of having a college education for my husband and children. What if she had been as selfish as I am?

I was driven from an early age to go after what I wanted—to accomplish more. In retrospect, I realize she sacrificed her life and her future for me so that I could be where I am right now.

I knew that my mother was depending on me to live her dream of having a perfect life in this not so perfect world. Consequently, I tried to be selective about the choices I made and the paths I chose, almost denying what really made me happy, as a means to an end.

I went to Georgia, Russia on a peace mission instead of attending my Junior Prom. What teenage girl in her right mind misses her first prom? Who does that?

I followed the normal course of events in life- finished high school, graduated with honors. I attended undergrad and barely graduated. I got married, had a baby, went to grad school, did remarkably well, and became a teacher, doing well at that.

I recently went back to school to earn my administrative certification in order to position myself for leadership opportunities within the school district. Now, I am beginning to believe that this decision and the time it took away from my family may have cost me my marriage.

My life is in fucking shambles.

AUGUST 13, 1997

I saw a face peering into my bedroom window today. When I turned for a closer look, it was gone. Maybe it was my imagination. I hope it was my imagination. Things have been so crazy around here lately that it is hard for me to distinguish what is real from what is fake.

Christian was on a business trip for the week in South Carolina and, quite frankly, I welcomed the solitude—well as much solitude as one could have with a little one crawling around. As I ran Ethan's bathwater, I thought about how Christian and I had been coexisting since the restaurant debacle with virtually no interaction. I thought about the fact that we had been sleeping apart for almost three months. Our once tender, loving, and passionate relationship had dissipated into one where I didn't touch him and he didn't touch me. His presence alone bothered me. Being around him bothered me.

I picked Ethan up and placed him in the tub. Happily, he giggled, kicked and splashed. Bath time was his favorite time of the day. It was our time together to sing and play with the many toys he had thrown into the tub. He was such a beautiful little human with big brown eyes and a head full of dark curly hair just like his father. His laugh and smile could brighten any room. I leaned down and nuzzled the crown of his head. The shampoo suds covered my nose. His hair smelled like baby shampoo. As Ethan splashed, I took a minute to wipe the shampoo suds off of my nose and look at myself —to actually look at myself. My caramel skin was dull, and my once big, vibrant hazel eyes looked tired and worn. The snazzy cut and hair color that had become my trademark looked unkempt and in desperate need of attention. My curves were withering away due to lack of attention, focus, and exercise. Outside of work, I was living in sweats, doing absolutely nothing to pull myself together. What was happening to me? Why was I allowing this situation, this man, to change who I was? I was losing myself.

Dear God, will the pain ever subside?

AUGUST 14, 1997

I saw the face in the window again today. This time it did not disappear. It lingered like it wanted me to see it... to recognize it. My heart was pounding in my chest like that of an animal being hunted. I frantically searched for the phone and immediately realized it was on the table closest to the window where the face was. I had to approach the window to get to the phone. What if they had a gun? The closer I got to the phone and the window, the farther the face shrank back and the more frightened I became. Why was she peering into my home? Why was she watching me?

I gathered Ethan into my arms, and grabbed the phone all in one swoop. Trembling, I dialed 911. By the time the operator answered, the face and the figure had retreated to the car that was parked, still running, outside of the house. She had lingered just long enough to ensure that I knew who it was.

"911, what is your emergency?"

"A woman. That woman from dinner a few months ago."

"What woman?" The operator's voice was calm and firm.

"My husband's girlfriend."

"Your husband's girlfriend? Ma'am, are you ok? Is anyone else in the house with you?"

"My son," I said. "My son is in the house with me."

"How old is your son, ma'am?"

"He's ten months old."

"We have dispatched officers to your home. Please stay on the line with me until they arrive."

I held the phone clutched in my hand as I waited for the police to arrive. The operator was as silent as I was while we waited.

The police arrived within five minutes. I explained the events of the last few months and the details of the last two days, telling them that the face appeared in the window yesterday and again today—that yesterday I thought I was mistaken, but today she let me recognize her. "She's sending me a message," I told them.

"What message, ma'am?"

"That she's not going away and she knows where we live."

The female officer kept peering out the window with cupped hands while the two male officers searched the house to make sure it was secure and that no one had gained entry. It was dark outside. "Are you going to do anything?" I asked. "This woman is clearly crazy."

She moved toward me and said, "I can understand your concern Mrs. Beck. I have to admit that this is very creepy behavior and we are concerned for you and your son's safety as well." The other two officers entered the living room and said, almost in unison, "She appears to be gone. The house is secure."

The female officer continued, "Since she has left the premises, unfortunately, there is not much we can do at this time."

The female officer tried to comfort me as best she could while explaining my options.

"Due to the volatile nature of the situation," she explained, "we advise you to place an emergency restraining order against her to protect Ethan and yourself. The order would declare that she could not physically be within five hundred feet of you or your son at any time."

I agreed, and after all of the paperwork was completed, I started to tremble again.

"We'll just hang around for a bit to see if she returns."

But after about an hour or so with no sign of Wynter, they left.

What the fuck had Christian gotten us into?

The woman was a damn fool. Who in their right mind would stalk their lover's wife and child? Clearly she was not in her right mind, because she was parked outside of my house, peering into my windows, looking at Ethan and me. What in the world was I going to do? I couldn't hold back the tears any longer.

Slowly, I sunk down to my knees on the floor and began to sob deeply. Never before had I felt this helpless, confused, and alone. Ethan, who had been playing with his toys nearby, crawled over, looked at me with those big beautiful eyes, and put his head on my knee. I gathered him up and cradled him in my arms, rocking us both to sleep there on the floor.

AUGUST 15, 1997

I woke up on the living room floor with Ethan in my arms, my cell phone chiming. I fumbled around quickly to answer it so as not to wake Ethan. "Hello," I whispered.

It was Christian.

"I was just calling to make sure you and Ethan are ok, and are up and moving around."

Christian normally dropped Ethan at school each morning, which allowed me time to ease into my seven thirty start at Briarwood High School with my eighth graders. It also gave Christian time to spend with Ethan, since he was normally asleep by the time Christian was finished with work each evening.

"We're up," I responded in a despondent tone.

Thank goodness it was Friday. Although preplanning for teachers had begun two weeks ago, this was the first week the kids were back to school from summer vacation and it had been challenging to say the least. It was always that way at the beginning of the school year when I got a new crop of kids. I had to train them or the entire year would be hell.

My classroom management philosophy was- *it's easier to loosen up than it is to tighten up* so, that meant I had to be mean as a hornet for the first month of school; no smiles, laughs or anything in order to set boundaries and expectations for my students. I had to teach them the rituals and routines for how our class would run, otherwise the students would make shit up and nine times out of ten, as the teacher, I would not like what they came up with. After a month, they knew my expectations and we were ready to rock and roll and enjoy each other for the rest of the school year.

Lord I wish it was still summer break, I thought to myself. I'm sure Christian called because he was missing his morning time with Ethan but also, I speculated, to point out the things that he did to "make my life easier."

The sound of Christian's voice brought back a flood of emotions and memories from the evening before. *I had to call the police.*

"Have you had that bitch in our home? Why does she know where we live?"

"Kami, what are you talking about? What do you mean?"

"Please don't act stupid Christian, like you didn't hear me or like you don't understand what I'm asking you. Have you had that bitch in our home?" I asked again this time my voice was elevated. "It's a simple question."

The silence between my question and Christian's response was brutal and deadly.

Tentatively Christian replied, "No, she hasn't been in our home, Kami. Why are you even asking me that?"

Frantically I hurried around the house with the phone between my shoulder and ear and Ethan on my hip. It was already six thirty, and I was running very late. On a normal day, by this time, I would be getting out of the shower and Christian would be getting Ethan ready to drop him at Ms. Richards's house.

"Kami." Christian said, his voice sharp and loud, "Talk to me. Tell me what's going on."

"Your crazy ass girlfriend has been spying on Ethan and me through the windows of the house for the past two nights. That's what's going on, Christian. I had to call the police last night." I ran out of breath. "What have you gotten us into? You had to go and fuck *the crazy bitch* and now she's stalking your family. The officers advised me to place an emergency restraining order against her to protect Ethan and me."

There was an audible gasp from Christian, followed by complete silence. His lack of response was sending me further into the unhealthy space I had occupied for the past four months.

"I gotta go, Christian. I just can't deal with you this morning. I have nothing left." I sighed.

"I'm on my way home," Christian responded.

By the time we hung up, it was already seven. There was no way I was in any kind of condition to teach children anything this morning. I needed to call the school and let them know that I had a family emergency and would not be able to come in today. I knew this was going to be a problem because every day of the first week of school is a critical day and you're not allowed to be absent. I nervously dialed the number to the school.

"Good Morning Ms. Thomas this is Ms. Beck. How are you this morning?"

"I'm fine Ms. Beck what's up?"

"I had a family emergency last night and I won't be able to make it in to school today."

"Ms. Beck, you know I can't approve an absence on a critical day. You're going to have to speak with Mr. Perry. Hold on a second, he is standing right here. Let me see if I can get his attention for you."

Mr. Perry was our school principal and I knew he was going to be upset. He never took kindly to teachers calling out. I didn't know what else to do. Unfortunately, this situation was beyond my control. I heard Ms. Thomas tell Mr. Perry, "It's Ms. Beck she *says* she had a family emergency last night."

Leave it to that heifer to start some shit. Why did she have to say it that way? Mr. Perry feeds off of her. If she is ok with it then he will be depending on how she delivers the information. Now, I knew he was going to trip. I would have to give him more information than I had planned in order for him to approve my absence. Lord, I didn't want everyone in the school knowing my business. Although I was talking to my principal and everything I shared with him was supposed to be confidential, I knew he was going to tell Ms. Thomas and she was going to tell the world. Ugh.

"Ms. Beck, how can I help you this morning?" Mr. Perry said sternly.

"Mr. Perry, I had a situation at my house last night where I had to have the police come out. Ethan and I are ok but, I am not going to be able to make it to school today."

"If you're ok and Ethan is ok, I don't understand why you're not going to be able to make it to school Ms. Beck."

"Sir, I have been having some problems at home since May. Last night, I had to take out a restraining order on an individual. I am in no condition to teach children today sir. I am sorry, but I am an emotional basket case right now."

"I see Ms. Beck. I am going to approve your absence but when you return to school I am going to need you to bring the restraining order paperwork as documentation. I have noticed a decline in your performance and I have to admit, I am concerned. Since you say that you have been having problems at home since the end of last school year then that kind of explains the timeline. I am going to need you to pull it together quickly or we may have to discuss your future at Briarwood."

I could not believe what I was hearing. My husband was cheating on me, a crazy bitch was stalking my son and me, and now my principal was threatening to fire me? Could things be any worse? I had just started my teaching career and was only in my second year. I didn't have tenure yet. He could fire me at the drop of a hat and I would have no recourse. I couldn't afford to get fired from my first teaching job.

Through tears I said, "Sir, I promise I will pull it together. Please just give me a chance. I will bring the paperwork to school with me on Monday so you can see I am not making this up. I wish I was making this up sir but unfortunately this is all happening to me."

"I will have Ms. Thomas submit your absence into Sub-Finder, Ms. Beck. Try to take care of yourself and Ethan and I will see you bright and early on Monday morning ma'am."

"Thank you Mr. Perry. I promise I will be there sir."

I thought about the last few months as I hung up the phone. Mr. Perry said he'd noticed a decline in my performance.

Where was that coming from? I'd been throwing myself relentlessly into work.

So I thought.

When I wasn't working, I was pouring my heart into my journal to cope and wrap my head around all I was experiencing.

Shortly after the Wynter incident, I'd decided to go back to school to work on my leadership certification. I had already completed my Master's degree in teaching secondary English, but needed to add on the leadership certification in order to get my career on an upward trajectory and apply for leadership positions.

I loved my students and the classroom, but teachers don't make enough money. I always knew I wanted to be a leader in education, and I felt like there was no time like the present to get 'er done as far as the credentials were concerned so that I would be ready when the right opportunity came along.

I didn't trust Christian as far as I could spit, and I wasn't about to become a broken-down statistic. I needed to get my ducks in a row so I could provide for Ethan and myself, since it was obvious that my somewhat young marriage was spiraling out of control. In fact, at this moment, everything in my perfect little world was falling completely apart.

By the time I got Ethan out of the bath and dressed it was seven thirty. Thankfully, Ms. Lovett, my favorite sub, had picked up my classes for the day. I was shook after speaking with Mr. Perry. So, the fact that Ms. Lovett would be with my kids put my mind at ease a bit. I hated missing school. My kids needed me but I really need this day to get my mind right. To reflect, relax, and pull myself together.

Classes at Oglethorpe start for me next week, and I have a few things that I need to take care of to prepare. Today would be the perfect day to take care of those things, spend some time in my thoughts, and plan my course of action. I quickly dabbed the excess cereal and peaches off of Ethan's beautiful little mouth, kissed him in my special spot between his cheek and his lips, grabbed him and his bag, and headed out the door for Ms. Richards's house.

SEPTEMBER 24, 1988

W hy did I always have to walk home?
I hated walking home from school, but I definitely was not going to catch the big cheese. On
Tuesdays and Thursdays it was either walk home or ride the
big cheese. Mama was busy taking my sisters to ballet, gym-
nastics, and swimming lessons, so, with all of *their* activities,
I had to walk home or take the cheese two days out of the
week. I couldn't wait to get my driver's license. Only two more
months to go and I would be able to drive myself wherever I
needed to go

The cars whizzed by as I contemplated my fate and lament-
ed over the fact that I was going to have to walk. There was no
other option. At the cue of the walk symbol in the crosswalk, I
hastily made my way across the stilled intersection before the
cars began to buzz again.

No sooner had I placed my foot on the curb of Kelley
Chapel then a car pulled up and began to slow next to me. I
had been walking home from school since August and had
grown accustomed to the obnoxious young boy call of "Hey

shawty" or the old man groan "Lookey here," so naturally I ignored the car and kept my chin up. I wanted no part in whatever they had in mind. I was just trying to get home safely.

"Kami," a scratchy but confident voice called.

I slowly looked over and caught a glimpse of "the guy." That guy. Him, the one that everyone was talking about. He was calling my name.

I grew even more perturbed with my mother for not picking me up from school today. Now, because of her, one of the *hottest* guys in the city was watching me as I walked down Kelley Chapel Road to my house. I was mortified that I was walking.

Damien Curry had made quite a name for himself—he and his brother, for that matter—for their association with the gang Down by Law. No one really knew if they were in Down by Law or just friends with the guys who made up one of the most infamous youth gangs in the South. It was clear he was from the other side of the tracks. What was not clear was how the hell he knew me.

I blurted out, "What do you want? Don't you see me trying to get home?"

"Yes, I can see you walking home. But I don't think you should be walking home, especially not alone."

"Is that so?" I said to him. "Thank you so much for your concern, kind sir. It baffles me as to why you care, or, for that matter, how you even know me."

"Know you? Every high school guy in DeKalb knows you."

"Huh? What are you talking about?"

"You have to know that you're one of the most beautiful girls in the world."

"Oh, here we go with the lines." I adjusted my backpack and quickened my pace.

"No seriously, you are. I've been trying to catch up with you since I saw you at the football game last week. That night I made up my mind that I was going to get to know you. I asked one of my boys to find out what he could about you, and he told me that you were one of the school's 'pride and joy' girls. So I came to campus to find you. "

"Pride and joy?" What the hell did he mean by that?

With all the grief the girls gave me at school every day, I certainly wasn't anyone's pride and joy, except for my Mama and Daddy. As he slowly cruised beside me, Damien explained that the guys at SWD prided themselves on the fact that they had some of the most beautiful girls in the city attending their school, and they often bragged about it. This caused problems for school administration, to say the least. There was always a steady stream of young men who did not belong on our campus coming to check out the "goods."

It was against district rules for students to be on campuses they did not attend. If Damien were caught, he would have been expelled. He currently attended Lakeside High School. I remembered hearing he had been kicked out of almost every high school in DeKalb County for fighting or some other disruptive behavior.

Merely being seen with him would be nothing but more trouble for me. Virtually every teenage girl at the school hated me already because their guys were always looking at me while they were walking them to class.

Just today, Lawrence, our star running back, had dropped his books because he was staring and didn't see the door divider before he ran into it.

Tamera, captain of the cheer squad, slapped him, threw me the finger, and said "Go be with her, since you lookin' so hard."

It was my junior year in high school and I was pretty much a loner, numb to this type of behavior. I had grown immune to the bullying and constant stares. In fact, for the most part, I didn't even realize when it was happening. And, I had given up on the possibility of ever having any female friends at my school. All of my friends attended other schools, and I was just fine with that.

I stilled my pace, turned toward the car, and looked Damien square in the face. He was seated inside a brand new, souped-up Volkswagen Rabbit. This was every teenage boy's dream car and his was set out to the nines—rims and all.

So here I was, Kami Papillon standing in front of the guy that all the girls wanted, while he was driving the car that all the guys wanted. I was looking directly into his face. Although he had a big reputation, Damien was small in stature. He couldn't have topped five eight. *How could someone so small cause so much trouble and wreak so much havoc,* I thought.

I could tell by the look in his eyes that my boldness took him aback. He was accustomed to intimidating most people, so this kind of fearlessness was something he rarely experienced. His brows were raised and his eyes were big, forming a questioning expression on his face—one of almost disbelief, but also intrigue.

People were constantly around him, at his beck and call. Why was he chasing me?

"Look," I said in a frustrated tone with my voice beginning to elevate. "What do you want from me? I'm a good girl, and I'm not interested in a bad boy. You're trouble, and Lord knows I don't need any more trouble or drama in my life. Now, if you could just be on your merry way, I would appreciate it."

"Ok, Miss Lady. Calm down," Damien said in a sly almost arrogant tone. "I will leave you to your walk."

I moved more quickly, hoping to leave him behind, but out of the corner of my eye, I saw that his car hadn't moved. He was literally sitting in the middle of the street watching me as I progressed home.

I prayed for him to be on his way. I didn't want him knowing where I lived. I started to make plans for dodging him.

I didn't know how I would explain our knowing each other if my parents found out about him following me home. Lord knows they would never approve of him.

After a few moments though, I heard the growl of his exhaust as he busted a U-turn in the middle of the street and headed back toward Wesley Chapel.

With relief, I released the breath that had been trapped in my lungs for the past ten minutes and continued my journey home. I thought about how he had exited gracefully and was happy that there was no further confrontation. I relaxed, not even realizing how tense I'd been.

As I turned onto my street, I looked up the road toward my house as I always did when I had to walk home. I think it was for reassurance that the journey was almost over.

Was I seeing things? I had to be seeing things.

The souped-up Volkswagen Rabbit was sitting in front of my house.

My stomach jumped into my throat so quickly I could taste my lunch. *How could he know where I lived?*

And if he had planned to come to my house uninvited, he could have just given me a ride. The nerve of him, to allow me to walk the rest of the way home as he sat waiting in front of my house.

Wait. I wasn't allowed company when my parents weren't at home. Although I was a junior in high school, my mother would absolutely kill me if she knew that a boy was at our house, especially without her being there. Panic set in quickly. It was already almost four. She and my sisters were just about to wrap up ballet class in downtown Decatur. They were always home by five. Damien had to go.

This was some shit. How was I going to get rid of him?

As I drew closer, I could see a huge smile on his face. My expression, however, did not match his. I was solemn and pissed on so many levels. First, he had let me walk without offering a ride. Second, he was parked in front of my house, and I hadn't told him where I lived. And third, he was about to get me into a world of trouble if he was still there when my mom came home.

My parents were strict. Something told me he already knew that, and parking in front of the house was part of his strategy to get me to talk to him.

"Look dude," I said as I approached. "I appreciate your persistence, I really do, but I need you to leave. If you're here when my mother gets home, I'm going to be in a world of trouble, and that will not bode well for you. I asked you back on Kelley Chapel what you wanted."

"Yeah, but you also did not give me an opportunity to respond. You went on a rant about not wanting any drama."

He was right. I hadn't given him a chance to respond.

"Ok, you have my attention. I'm listening," I said praying we could get this over with and he would leave.

"You have two sisters. Your dad is in the car business and your mother doesn't work. Her world revolves around her family."

I shifted the weight of my backpack from one side to the other to provide myself some relief and balance as I wondered how he knew these things about me.

"You're on the swim team and swim the breast stroke. In fact, you hold the fastest recorded time in the state."

I was becoming uncomfortable as he continued to rattle off details of my life and my family. Is this what gang members did? Try to get into your head before they go in for the kill?

"You don't talk to many people and have a really hard time with the girls at school," he said. "They hate you because you're pretty, yet you don't really act like a pretty girl. That's what drew me to you. As beautiful as you are, you speak to and you smile at everyone, even if they don't speak and smile back. I have never seen or met anyone like you."

I stood there in front of my house, stunned.

"I asked around about you, but the only way I could get to know you is by talking to you. So, here I am. And now you won't talk to me. What's going on?"

I thought about Damien's question. I really didn't know much about him—only the things I had heard others say. What gave me the right to judge him?

"So," Damien said, "my plan is to sit here until you talk to me. You interest me. I want you to know about me. More than the street committee knows," he said with a chuckle.

I smiled back, despite my misgivings.

By the time he finished his soliloquy it was nearly five p.m. Surely my mother and sisters would be rounding the corner of our street any second now. I had no choice but to give him my phone number. I knew he wouldn't leave unless he had it. I thought about giving him the wrong number, but knew he would just come back.

I tore a small piece of paper from my notebook and quickly scribbled the number, then handed it to him. As he took the paper from my hand, he grabbed my fingers.

I looked at him until he let my hand drop. Without saying goodbye, he punched the accelerator and headed for the end of the street, leaving me standing in shock at the mailbox, watching his car roar toward Kelley Chapel.

As he turned left, my mother and my sisters turned right onto the street. I quickly pulled my thoughts together as I checked the mailbox. After gathering the mail, I jumped into the van with my smiling mom and rowdy sisters for a ride to the backdoor.

"Kami," they all shouted in unison.

"How was your day?" Mama asked.

"Just peachy." I replied.

"Peachy, huh? Interesting word choice. What did you learn at school today?" she probed further. She always asked this as a follow-up question when we were not forthcoming with information.

"How to start a fire." I grinned.

"I'm being serious, Kami."

"I am too, Mama. You should be receiving a call from my biology teacher."

All of a sudden it was quiet in the van. It was never quiet in the van. I felt my Mama's eagle-eyed stare on the side of my face, burning a hole in my cheek. My sisters and I knew that a call from a teacher with anything other than a compliment was a no-no on all fronts. Coupled with the fact that I had said it so calmly, things were not looking good for me.

"Kami, why would Mr. Prince have a reason to call me?"

"I don't know, Mama. The same reason he opted to put chemicals he did not want us to mix on the table together in front of a bunch teenagers, I guess."

Mr. Prince was a new teacher and he wasn't the brightest bird. He never thought things all the way through.

"Stop being a smartass. I'm gonna need you to tell me what happened. You know I can't stand surprises, and the rule in this house is that I don't want anyone telling me about my children. I want you to tell me about you. Now start telling."

"Mama, Mr. Prince put four vials of chemicals on our group's lab table and asked us not to touch the vials or mix the chemicals together until we received further directions. Hampton and Heath are in my lab group. You know them. They are always looking for ways to get a laugh out of people, so, as Mr. Prince distributed supplies to the other groups, the chemicals on our table got mixed. I didn't do it. In fact, I didn't even see it happen, because I was talking to Shane."

Shane was one of the only girls I talked to at school. She was seated at the lab table behind mine.

"Since I was in the group and no one would snitch, I got in trouble too."

My mother stared at me for a moment, her eyes narrowing as she drove our van up the driveway to the back of the house. "You guys could have killed yourselves."

I nodded my head in agreement as my mind drifted back to my encounter with Damien. He didn't seem like a gang member. Quietly, my interest was piqued. I wondered how long he would wait to call.

AUGUST 19, 1997

It's our second anniversary. Christian always gives really nice gifts, and since he is in the doghouse, I expect him to go all out. Wonder what I'm going to get?

As far as dinner goes, I know where we won't be going.

He won't be getting a damn thing from me, and I'm certain he knows that. Happy Fucking Anniversary.

AUGUST 21, 1997

It's me, it's me, it's me, oh Lord,
Standing in the need of prayer.
It's me, it's me, it's me, oh Lord,
Standing in the need of prayer...

The bubbles danced as the words of the spiritual played over and over in my mind. I sank farther into the tub. What a long day. What a long forty-eight hours. Hell, for that matter, what a long six months.

The stillness of the room and the movement of the water comforted me as I soaked my tired body. In the near distance, I heard Christian and Ethan in their customary game of chase. Ethan's deep, guttural laugh made my heart smile for a moment before thoughts of that woman watching us through the windows of my home crept into my mind.

I can't believe she was watching us. *Geez.*

With a swirl of the bathwater, I released that thought and caught a glimpse of my wrist, now adorned with a six-carat channel-set diamond bracelet.

Christian did buy amazing gifts, but it was going to take way more than this bracelet for him to get back into my good graces. I had vehemently refused to go to dinner with him for our anniversary.

When asked I responded sarcastically, "Hell no, I'm not going out to dinner with you. What do we have to celebrate? Another one of your women may pop up on me. You and Wynter have already made it so I will never go to Pano's and Paul's again. Pretty soon restaurants won't be an option for us."

I'd also stuck to my guns about not getting him anything. Why should I?

I, however, woke up to a card and a rectangular jewelry box that contained the bracelet that was now on my wrist. It was far too beautiful to throw at him or give back, so, I decided the best place for it was my wrist. Hell, I definitely deserved it.

A hard knock on the front door, followed by two quick rings of the doorbell, interrupted my thoughts. Our home was small, which meant you could hear everything that was happening no matter where you were in the house – even if you were lounging in the bathroom.

I slid further into the water, confident that Christian and Ethan would greet our guest. This was my first moment of peace all day, and I was not expecting company, so I was completely disinterested in whoever was visiting.

There was another knock, followed by two additional rings of the doorbell.

Christian and Ethan were putting up such a ruckus they must not have heard the door.

"Christian." I yelled from the bathroom. No response. "Christian," I yelled again. *Why couldn't they hear the door?*

Realizing my relaxing soak was at an end, I surged out of the water, donned my robe, and headed to the front door. I peeked out of the side window. *What were the police doing here?* I opened the door just as the officer was about to knock for the third time.

"May I help you, officer?"

"Yes ma'am, are you Mrs. Beck?"

"Yes officer, I am."

"Is Mr. Beck in?"

"Yes officer, he is."

"Can you ask him to come to the door, please?"

"He's in the back with our son. Is there something I can help you with?"

"No ma'am, I need to speak with Mr. Beck."

Anxiety and tension mounted in my stomach, and bile rose in my mouth. I trembled.

Sensing my concern, the officer said, "I just need to talk to him."

They were in Ethan's room in full play wrestle flow, screaming and laughing. No wonder they couldn't hear.

"Christian, the police are here."

Christian's face was a blank. He didn't seem to react in any way, he just looked at me.

He gathered himself off the floor, handed Ethan to me, and headed for the door.

I was dead on his heels because I knew I needed to hear it all—the entire conversation. Christian lied, and if I didn't hear it from the officer, I would never know the real story.

As I rounded the corner, I heard the officer say, "Mr. Beck, you have been charged with assault. This serves as your official notice of these charges. Do you understand?"

"Yes," Christian said.

"You have a beautiful family, sir. Out of respect for them, because they are here with you, and because you were not physically present when these allegations against you were made, it is not my intent to take you in this evening. You are commanded to appear in court two weeks from today to respond to these charges. Do you understand, sir?"

"Yes," Christian responded.

In utter shock, I stood speechless in the doorway of the foyer, holding Ethan, who was squirming and whining, trying to get back to his father and their game.

Christian was too calm. His demeanor confirmed this visit was not a surprise. *He knew they were coming.* What the hell had he done?

Christian closed the door and gestured ever so calmly for Ethan.

I didn't know what to do. My feet were glued to the floor and the signals from my brain to my limbs had stopped. I couldn't move. Confused, I held on to Ethan tightly and said, "Assault Christian? You've just been charged with assault and you're walking around here cool as a cucumber? Are you crazy? So, you're running around beating people up now? Is that what you're doing? Who are you? Who are you becoming?"

Refusing to hand Ethan over, I stepped back from Christian. Angrily, he moved forward and said in a stern tone, "Give me my son."

"I will not." I screamed. "Not until you answer my questions. Who did you assault Christian? When did this happen? Why did you do this?" I demanded.

"Kami. This is none of your fucking business." Christian screamed. "I will handle it now, hand me my God Damn son."

Christian never yelled. He was always so cool and collected. Nothing ever seemed to faze him.

Ethan began to cry as Christian and I tussled. Christian's pinky caught the diamond bracelet he had just given me for our anniversary. The bracelet snapped in half and fell to the floor. I looked down at the bracelet in shock as Christian lunged forward tearing Ethan from my arms.

Christian had gone stark mad. He was crazy like his fucking girlfriend. They were both flocked.

In tears, I sunk down to the floor in the foyer as Christian stomped down the hallway back to our son's room. What was happening to us?

NOVEMBER 18, 1988

The phone rang at exactly midnight.

""Happy birthday, baby." Damien's sweet, raspy voice crooned through the phone sending shock waves through me. I liked his voice. It was easy to listen to- a perfect tenor and, although he didn't sing, it was melodic in tone.

"I wanted to be the first person to tell you that on your special day."

"Thank you." I had been waiting on his call. "Hell," I told myself, "he'd better call me on my birthday. That's what *boyfriends* are supposed to do."

Despite my parents' disapproval, Damien and I had become quite the item over the past couple of months.

"He's not at all like people say," I would tell my mom. "He works at Little Caesar's and goes to school."

"Really, you think slinging pizza pays for all those toys?" She refused to listen to my arguments.

"He's got a bad reputation, and you're going to get a bad reputation by hanging around with him," Daddy would tell me.

I was proud of him. I knew that contrary to popular belief, his long hours accounted for his toys—the clothes, the sneakers, and the car.

"If you lay in the bed with dogs Kami you will get fleas," Mama would say.

"You may not know everything about him honey. Just be careful. These boys are only after one thing Kami. I'm not sure about Damien. Protect yourself baby. Protect your heart," Daddy would say.

"Where are you," I asked him, eager for him to come by.

Just leaving work. I have something for you."

"What is it?"

"I'm not going to tell you that."

"I know, but it was worth a try," I said, trying to play the disappointed role. We both laughed.

"I want to see you," I said.

"I'm on my way to pick you up." He chuckled.

"You know I live in Fort Knox. If I try to leave the house, sirens and all kinds of shit go off."

I was surprised my parents hadn't come roaring in already, Mama telling me it was too late to be on the phone.

"Lord knows," I added, "if they knew it was you on the phone, they would have a flat-out hissy fit."

He chuckled, and then I remembered I was babysitting my sisters and they were already sound asleep. I was alone. How could I have forgotten? I was so busy waiting by the phone for my birthday call.

"I know why Mama's not on me about being on the phone," I said. "Her and Daddy are at the annual Automotive Dealer's Awards Ceremony and won't be back until well after two.

"I'll be right over," Damien said.

It was the perfect opportunity to be alone with him, but I was afraid. I'd never even thought about sneaking anyone into the house before, but obviously Damien had.

"Your bedroom's at the front of the house, I can just open the window and climb through," he'd told me one time.

I'd giggled and brushed him off.

"Come on, Kami," he was coaxing.

"One of my sisters could wake up, or decide to crawl into bed with me. That has been happening regularly with Dia. *Prezy*, her version of the "Boogie Man", has been haunting her and waking her up out of her sleep so often that Mama is considering taking her to the doctor. And Lord knows she has a big mouth, Damien. Mama and Daddy would know you were over here before she finished her cheese toast in the morning."

"It's your birthday, and I want to deliver my gift in person," Damien said. "There's never going to be a better time."

"My parents will kill me, and my dad would shoot you," I said.

I played with the phone, listening to Damien talking about how he could be over, how much we deserved to be together, how we'd have a few minutes alone for a change.

I was a good girl, but my parents treated me like they didn't trust me. They were so overprotective. All of my other friends went to places like Six Flags, the mall, the movies, and on coed dates, while I was stuck in the house babysitting my sisters.

When they did allow me out, they made me take my sisters. Ugh.

"I have absolutely no life," I complained.

I envied Damien and the others who had all the independence in the world. If I'd let myself think about it, my inaccessibility was probably part of his attraction to me.

"I know, honey," Damien responded.

"What if we get caught?" I said.

"We won't get caught, babe. I just want to give you your birthday present. I won't be there long, my dad said I have to be home by one thirty."

I looked at my watch. It was already a quarter after twelve.

"Ok, only for a few minutes. How long is it going to take you to get here?" I asked as a scurried around trying to straighten up the living room. Dia and Lynie had toys all over the place. But wait, this wasn't a typical visit like the ones we had when Mama and Daddy were home, I thought. I couldn't just have Damien out in the living room. What if one of my sisters got up? There would be no place for me to hide him. At least in my room I could put him in the closet or something. Yea, the bedroom is definitely better I reconciled. We'll just sit on my bed. Nothing bad.

"I'm literally right around the corner from you, and already rollin' that way. Five minutes, maybe."

"Ok, when you get here, come to the front of the house instead of the back, and knock on my window. I don't want to wake Ginger. If she hears or sees anything out of the ordinary, she will start all that barking, and that will definitely wake Dia."

Ginger was our feisty Pomeranian, who looked sweet, but would bite your hand off if you touched her. She never bit anyone in our family, but if a stranger came at her, it was amazing how quickly she would attack and then go back to looking like she had no idea what had occurred.

When I heard his gentle knock on my window. I opened the blinds and held my finger up, motioning to Damien that I would be at the front door in one minute.

I tiptoed through the hallway so as not to wake my sisters. The old wood floors of the house always creaked at any movement, and tonight was no exception. It was almost as if they were telling on me…telling on us.

My room was close to the front door—literally on the other side of a wall that separated my bedroom from the living room. I quietly opened the door and there stood Damien with a slice of cookie cake, a single rose, and a Macy's shopping bag.

I peered into the bag. The box inside looked as though it had been wrapped by Damien himself.

I motioned him inside, closed the door behind him, and put my finger to my lips. "Shh," I warned. Then I quietly led him to my bedroom.

He raised his brows.

"It's safer in my bedroom," I whispered.

Once securely inside, I hugged him tightly, and he gave me a gentle kiss on the lips.

"Hey baby," Damien whispered as he broke our embrace and pushed me back so he could look at my face. "Happy birthday, beautiful."

"Thank you," I replied, thinking, "There's something about him that just makes me, ohhhhh."

"Are these for me?" I asked in an excited tone, pointing to the items in his arms. There's something about the anticipation before opening a gift that gives me a rush. I always look at gifts as being glimpses into a person's soul—into their thoughts and feelings about you. I couldn't wait to see what the box revealed about Damien's feelings about me.

"Who else would they be for?" Damien had a mischievous smile on his face, and his tone was sarcastic. I smirked as he placed the rose and the slice of cake on the edge of my bed and handed me the shopping bag. I took the box out of the bag and laid it on the bed next to the rose and cake. After carefully inspecting the wrapping, I looked up at Damien and we giggled.

"Hey, it was the best I could do." Damien smiled and shrugged.

I gently tugged at the ribbon that loosely surrounded the box. It looked as though it had been tied like a shoestring. I then carefully but strategically pulled at the edges of the wrapping paper, which barely covered the box. It was the thought that counted. Right? I could tell by all the tape that this was clearly Damien's best as far as wrapping went. I smiled at him.

He was watching intently, beaming with pride over his work.

Finally, after getting through all of the paper and tape, I lifted the lid of the box. I saw a delicate green strap peeking out from under the white tissue paper. I reached my hand under the paper, pulled the bag out and laid it on my lap. The supple green leather donned the famous interlocking G pattern that was forever Gucci's trademark. For the last few months, I had been drooling over the bright green bag each time we walked by the window of Macy's during our secret mall meetings.

I looked up at Damien and trembled. Never did I imagine I would own this bag. "You shouldn't have. It's…it's gorgeous."

Damien's smile beamed from ear to ear.

He had gotten the exact response he was going for from the gift.

Suddenly, a sadness came over me. I know Damien could tell because his smile faded.

"What's wrong, Kami?"

"My Mama and Daddy are never going to allow me to accept this."

"Well, why not?"

"It's way too expensive, and they have never allowed me to accept gifts from boys. They believe that when you get gifts like this, it's because you're doing something that you're not supposed to be doing."

"Huh?"

"Like sex, Damien. My parents are going to think that if you're buying me gifts like this, I'm giving it up."

"Well, I wish that were true," he said with a chuckle. "There have been no home runs here. You have only allowed me to second and perhaps third base."

I cut my eyes at him and playfully smacked him on the arm.

"Be serious, stupid."

"Ok, ok." Damien responded, trying to straighten up. "You have a job. Tell them you've been saving up and finally had enough to buy it for your birthday. They don't have to know I bought it for you. Only we need to know that."

"You're right."

I did have a job, and it wasn't out of character for me to save up for things I really wanted. It was a brilliant plan. I smiled at him. He could be so smart and calculated at times. I knew this all too well as I reminisced about the day we'd met, when he'd allowed me to walk all the way home, only to find him parked in front of my house. Humph. I was so done with him that day. But here we were, months later, standing in my bedroom on my birthday as a couple.

I looked up at Damien with a big smile on my face and gently wrapped my arms around his neck. "You did good, babe. Thank you so much for the beautiful purse. I really appreciate it." Damien wrapped his arms around my waist and pulled me toward him. He gently kissed me on my nose and then my lips.

I kissed him back. I could feel his nature rising in his pants, and for a second it startled me. I tried to back away from him a bit.

Instead of allowing me to flee as I normally did, Damien pulled me closer and gently slid his tongue in between my lips. I opened my mouth to receive him. There was an unfamiliar feeling mounting in the bottom of my stomach—kinda like the feeling you get when you're scared, but different.

Damien gently backed me up onto my bed as he continued to kiss me slowly.

I had been resisting his advances for months, only allowing him to kiss and finger fuck me, but this evening, I felt different. I felt adventurous, and I was curious about what he looked like *down there*. I wasn't sure if I wanted to go all the way, but was feeling like I wanted to go farther than I had ever before.

As we lay across the bed, I could feel his manhood growing and pressing hard against my private place. Why was it so hard? He gently slid his hand into my pants and moved my panties to the side. He used his index finger to stroke my top and his middle and ring fingers to slide in and out of me. My body was getting hot and that feeling inside my stomach was growing more and more intense. As he continued to stroke, he whispered in my ear, "I wanna feel you, Kami."

"You're feeling me," I responded.

"Not with my fingers, with him."

"I'm scared, Damien. I've never gone all the way before. Is it going to hurt?"

"I'll go slow. I promise."

"Do you **have** a condom?" I asked.

Damien shifted to his side, pulled out his wallet, and slid out a small, square, blue package.

"Do you always carry those?" I smirked, despite my nervousness.

"No, babe, of course not. Tonight I wanted to be prepared just in case you were ready or had pity on me."

I smiled as I rolled over and began to pull the sheets back on my bed.

Damien lifted his body and we both slid inside the warm covers.

Although I had a smile on my face, my mind was racing. *Is this it? Is this how your first time happens?*

Damien slowly began to kiss me again—first on the nose, then on the cheeks, and then on the mouth. He was doing what he said, going slow.

I could tell by looking at him that this moment was as important to him as it was to me.

He slid his tongue into my mouth again, and I received him. Instead of sliding his hand into my pants and panties, this time, he gently began to pull them down and off. After he pulled mine off, he proceeded to take his off, and then returned to lie by my side.

He gazed at me and softly asked, "You ready, baby?"

I nodded my head. *We were going all the way tonight.*

Damien positioned himself over me. He lifted my sweatshirt and gently began to caress and suck both of my breasts.

That unfamiliar yet familiar feeling returned, warming me from the depth of my stomach.

He rose to his knees. With this motion I could see his full manhood in perfect view. *It's huge. How is that going to fit inside me?* I began to panic as I watched Damien slide the condom over himself and check for air pockets, as we had learned in sex education class. My legs began to tremble, but I refused to be a punk. I was doing this tonight.

Damien went back to kissing my breasts. His manhood now out of sight, and coupled with the sensations of his touch, I was comforted, and my body began to submit.

I felt his fingers traveling down my stomach to explore my special place. He rubbed my clit and I began to feel wetness between my legs. My stomach was on fire, and my special place was preparing itself, dripping, opening, and throbbing.

Damien positioned himself so that the tip of his manhood was at my opening. Then he slowly entered me, first the tip, and then with each subsequent stroke, he went deeper and deeper, giving me more and more of his manhood.

The initial sting of penetration subsided and had been replaced by a delicious feeling of fullness. My body relaxed in this carnal space, completely submitting to his tempo, stroke by stroke, expanding, gripping, and dancing to the music of our flow.

SEPTEMBER 17, 1997

The heavy stainless steel doors of the elevator jerked closed to carry us to our courtroom on the fourth floor. Packed to capacity with other individuals whom I'm guessing had similar shenanigans going on in their lives, the elevator struggled to lift each group to their respective floors.

The air and silence grew staler and thicker as we ascended.

When we finally made it to our floor, Carl motioned Christian and me into a huddle to brief us on strategy and what was about to occur. "As we previously discussed, it's very important that both of you maintain your composure throughout this hearing," Carl advised. "I realize this is a very sensitive situation and emotions are high for both of you right now. Wynter will be here, Kami, so please try not to engage her in any way."

I mean, who was this hearing for? Surely not me. Although Carl was representing both of us, I was getting perturbed as he explained how important it was for the judge to see us as a happy family, and Wynter as an individual who was stalking us and trying to dismantle that family unit.

"Christian, you may have to admit the affair in court. This judge is no fool, and stands on the grounds that most of the time there is some sort of relationship that existed prior to the onset of the stalking behavior. I plan to address this head-on to throw the prosecution off and gain the judge's trust right up front. Do either of you have an issue with this approach?"

Christian and I both shook our heads.

In fact, I was looking forward to seeing Christian squirm in front of the judge regarding his transgressions against our marriage.

Carl continued, "Christian, in your comments, you are to state that when you decided to break off the affair and fix things in your marriage, Wynter became furious and vowed to ruin your life."

This was my first time hearing this part. I had never gotten the details around how Christian had "ended it" with Wynter, or how the police ended up at our house that night subpoenaing him to court.

Carl was claiming that Christian's act was one of self-defense, and that the only reason he had visited Wynter was to tell her to stay away from his family. Since there were no witnesses to Wynter's alleged assault by Christian, Carl was confident that her charges against Christian would be dropped, but that our stalking charges would stick, thus resulting in immediate deportation back to Somalia for Wynter.

Apparently, Christian knew that Wynter had planned to do something to retaliate against him, and the first step in her plan was to make regular visits to our home and stalk Ethan and me.

What she had not considered was that stalking was apparently immediate grounds for deportation, which was the exact angle that Carl and Christian were pursuing. The restraining order I had filed against her was the single most important piece of evidence they had to cement their claim and negate the charges that had been filed against Christian.

What I wanted to know was why Christian hadn't warned me. I was seething with anger. The thought that Christian knew there was a possibility that this woman was going to come after his family and he had not said anything pissed me off. I had a good mind to leave his lying, deceitful ass right there and foil this whole goddamn plan. I began to take some deep breaths in order to calm myself. I knew that, if I did leave, that decision would only harm Ethan and me further. Although I worked, Christian was the primary provider for our family. I needed time to decide what I was going to do. If I was going to leave, I needed an exit strategy.

"Kami, are you ok?' Carl asked.

"I'm fine, Carl," I said, sarcasm dripping from my words. "I'm just wondering why Christian didn't care to share Wynter's threats with me, that's all." I cut my eyes at Christian, who was looking at me, "I didn't need you overreacting or adding fuel to the fire," Christian snapped back. Things were getting pretty tense in the room.

Before I could get my response to Christian out, Carl said, "Look, I need you two to hold it together until we get out of here. If all goes as planned, this should be over in forty-five minutes tops, and Kami, you can tear into Christian then. But right now, if you two want a positive result out of this, you need to pull it together and act like you love each other." With that, Carl turned away from us and led us into the courtroom.

Wynter was already inside, seated with her attorney at a long wooden table on the right side. They were in deep conversation when she noticed us enter the room. Her eyes were ablaze; not in an angry way, but passionate. This marked the first time I was truly able to get a good look at her. It had been dark in the restaurant the evening we met for the first time, and her face and figure had been hard to fully make out through the curtains that covered the living room windows.

Her eyes jumped obsessively from Christian to me and back to Christian, taking in our every movement. Before I had an opportunity to fully size her up, we had arrived at our space and the bailiff was at the front of the courtroom saying, "All rise. The second judicial court is now in session, Honorable Judge Martin presiding."

The proceedings went off without a hitch—just as Carl had predicted.

Wynter let out an audible gasp when the judge ordered her detained for immediate deportation. I felt sorry for her for a second, until I began to recall what her actions had done to my family. Things would never be the same, and I knew it.

I had not, however, expected them to take her into immediate custody, and, judging from the look on her face, she hadn't either.

In order to get Wynter to the holding room they had to pass our table and she was not going down without a fight. Wynter bucked around like a wild animal while they attempted to restrain her arms and legs. Once she was finally cuffed, they began to move her from the courtroom. In one final lunge she spun around to look me in my face and smirked, "I may be gone physically, but a part of me will always be with Christian."

Before I could contain myself, I blurted out, "Bitch, you will never be what I am to him. Don't you see that they are about to ship your ass back to Somalia? You were just a jump-off used to occupy his time when I was unavailable. The problem is, you didn't know your place."

The words melted off my lips so quickly I didn't have time to retract. As they oozed, a weight lifted off of my spirit. Although she had not acted alone, I could no longer bite my tongue. Christian and this bitch had completely turned my life upside down.

Wynter's body caved, forcing the guards to carry her the rest of the way to the holding room.

Christian stood in shock, much like he had that evening in the restaurant.

Up to now, I had been almost mute about the subject, but Wynter's statement had taken me over the edge. I had been dying to address her since that evening at Pano's and Paul's, since she'd ruined my Mother's Day dinner celebration, and subsequently my marriage.

Through clenched teeth Christian whispered, "Just like I said Kami, you're adding fuel to the fire."

With daggers in my eyes, I swung around to face him and said, "If you knew how to control your bitches, we would not be here in court today."

Carl, sensing things were about to go real bad real quick, shoved us out of the courtroom into a small conference room next to the elevators.

The room was tight but thank goodness it was empty. "You got me having to take out restraining orders and shit to keep your hoes from stalking me and Ethan in our own home," I told Christian, wagging my finger in his face. "What the fuck do you think this is? You put my life and your son's life in danger on so many levels, and you have the gall to tell me that I'm adding fuel to the fire?"

Christian's eyes were bucked and his caramel skin had turned blood red. I assume he was fire engine mad but I didn't give a fuck. Carl moved between us to serve as a living shield in case someone decided to through a blow.

"I'm sick of your shit Kameleon," Christian screamed with his fists clenched.

"You're sick?" I screamed back. "You're the one who failed to teach that whore rule number one: *Know your place.* You allowed her to believe the dream—that she could have my life. And look at you, still protecting her. What about me, Christian? When are you ever going to protect me?"

Carl gently grabbed me, pulling me out of Christian's face before I had a chance to haul off and slap the shit out of him.

He had already resolved one issue today, and I guess he wasn't looking to bail me out of jail for assault in a federal building. He took me into the elevator with him and asked Christian to take the next elevator down to allow some space and time for me to calm down.

As the elevator doors closed, I said, "I don't know who the fuck he thinks I am." Before I could blink it back, a tear sprinted down my cheek. Many others quickly joined that one tear. Before I knew it, I was in full cry. Carl held me tight in the elevator as I sank into his arms and allowed the tears to flow;

releasing all of the anger, pain, and humiliation I had felt over the last several months; releasing Christian and Wynter through the salt of my tears.

DECEMBER 16, 1988

T
hank goodness today is an early release day from school.
I dropped my backpack at the foot of the bed and climbed on top of the soft comforter. My stomach was killing me and my insides were all twisted up. Every time I went to the bathroom, it felt like my bottom was going to fall out. *What the hell was going on?* As I shifted to my side, the phone rang.

"Hello."

"Hey babe, how was your day?" Damien said.

"Fine," I grimaced as my stomach twisted.

"Everything ok?"

"My stomach is killing me."

"Is it that time of the month?"

"Ummm, no. Wait, what's today?"

"December fifth, babe."

I thought for a second and then realized I had not seen any signs of Red Man since the last week in October. And we were in December. My breath began to quicken and my heart raced as I scoured my mind. *Had this ever happened before?* Red

Man came like clockwork every month, during the last week of each month. I was never late. No, I had never missed my cycle before. With ice-cold fingers I clutched the phone to my chest- forgetting Damien was on the phone. Was I pregnant? How could that be possible? We'd only done it once and we'd used a condom. I'd watched him put it on.

"Babe, is everything ok?"

"I don't know, Damien, I missed my cycle last month."

There was dead silence on the phone.

All of a sudden, I heard a familiar rustling through the line, paired with my mother's shaky, fragile voice.

"Kami, hang up the phone and come to my room. Now."

She listened in on us. How had we not heard her pick up the phone?

Suddenly, like a volcanic eruption, I leaned over the side of my bed and began vomiting profusely. My body trembled with anxiety and fear at the thought of being pregnant at sixteen and having to talk to my parents.

Damien's voice came from the phone, lying on the floor, "Kami, are you ok?"

Without as much as a goodbye, I hung up the phone, leaving Damien's question unanswered. I didn't know if I was okay.

I suppose my mother heard me vomiting, because before I could make it to her room, she was standing at my bedside with the trash can in her hands, cupping my hair and holding my neck up at the same time, to keep vomit off the comforter.

With all the commotion, Dia and Lynie raced into the room with baby dolls in tow. "Girls, go to your room. Now," Mama scolded. Mama was serious, Dia and Lynie backed their way out of my room as quickly as they had entered. After a final heave emptied the remaining contents of my stomach, I looked up at my mother. She was crying.

"Kami, what have you done, baby?"

The sound of her voice alone caused my eyes to pool and tears to sprint down my cheeks like Flo Jo on hurdles. The heaviness of her tone and the overwhelming sadness in her eyes let me know that this hit her like a ton of bricks. As protective as she'd been, watching my every move, not allowing me to attend certain functions or hang around certain people, she still had not been able to save me.

"Kami, this is what I was warning you about. This is what I feared would happen with you dating Damien. Part of the reason I dislike him so is because I see some of your father's ways in him. He's a flashy fast talker just like Jordan. I feel like I'm eighteen all over again except it's my baby girl that is in trouble this time instead of me. If you're pregnant honey, you're going to have to make the same decision I did. I've certainly made my share of mistakes. I never wanted you to have to go through what I went through. I tried to keep you as close to me as possible. You can't imagine how much this hurts honey. I have tried so hard to protect you and now this." Mama's voice cracked as she cried holding her ivory face in her hands.

After a few seconds, Mama looked up and asked, "When was your last cycle, baby?"

Terrified, I struggled to find strength, and finally crackled out, "The end of October."

Mama dropped her head and said, "Missing your cycle is the first indication of pregnancy, honey. Why didn't you tell me?"

"Mama, I didn't even realize until today. Things have been so busy over the past month with my birthday and our trip to Baton Rouge that I lost track until today, talking to Damien."

"Kami, your Daddy and I warned you about that boy from the start."

"It wasn't that I was trying to hide anything from you or anyone, Mama, I just didn't know."

"How long have you been sexually active? When did this happen?" Mama asked.

My stomach was in knots. Mama and I had never really had this kind of conversation before. All she had ever told me was, "You better not do it." So, until my birthday, I had not.

How could I tell her I'd had Damien in her house while she and Daddy were gone? She was never going to trust me again.

"Mama, I swear I only did it once, the night of my birthday."

"Kami, once is all it takes. Wait, this happened the night of your birthday? The night your Daddy and I were at the ball and we left you here to babysit?" Mama jumped up from the bed and began pacing the floor of my bedroom. "Kami, how could you do that? How could you betray our trust like that? You know the rule – no company in this house when we're not here," Mama scolded. "I am so disappointed in you."

I curled my body into a tight little ball and began to sob and rock back and forth. I felt so hopeless. I tried to calm and comfort myself by holding on as tight as I could.

Mama finally lowered her voice and moved closer to me. She put her arm around me and said, "Come on baby, we will get through this. You know your father is going to have a fit, Kami. I have to figure out a way to tell him and keep him from killing that boy."

I hadn't even thought about Daddy. Mama knowing had been bad enough. "I may as well just kill myself now," I thought, "Life is over."

I sobbed at the thought of how upset and disappointed Daddy was going to be when he found out. *Why hadn't I just listened?* I should never have gone all the way with Damien.

"Mama, I swear we used protection. I don't know how this could have happened."

"Kami, are you sure he put it on?"

"I watched him do it."

"Well, sometimes condoms break, baby, but that is neither here nor there. At this point, it is what it is. We need to confirm whether you're pregnant or not. Watch your sisters for a minute while I run to the drugstore to pick up a home pregnancy test."

It seemed like Mama was back to the house in two seconds flat. I barely had a chance to breathe and decompress before she was ushering me into her bathroom, the little pink box under her arm.

"Kami, I need you to pee on this."

I pulled down my pants and panties and sat on the toilet. I was so uncomfortable, but I knew Mama wasn't about to leave the bathroom until she knew what was going on. So, I prayed and peed, hoping that by some miracle the pregnancy test was negative.

Before I could pull my pants up all the way, a bright pink plus sign had formed on the indication window of the test. The results served as confirmation that this was real. At the age of sixteen, I was pregnant.

Test in hand, Mama and I exited the bathroom and sat on the edge of her bed. Mama's expression was heavy. Bags had begun to form under her eyes from all the tears. And her lips were pursed in a straight line.

"Baby, I never wanted you to have to make the same decisions that I did," Mama said quietly. "Though I love you with every ounce of my being, when I decided to have you, my decision cost me my college dreams. It cost me the future I had planned for myself. I don't regret my decision at all, because you and your sisters are the most beautiful things that have happened in my life. In fact, you and your sisters are my life. But I wanted more for you."

I sat next to her with my head bowed. Listening intently.

"When your grandfather found out I was pregnant, he said, 'Avery, you're going to have to make a choice I am either paying for college or a wedding. Which is it going to be because I can't do both.' Back in those days if you had a baby in our family, you got married. There was no such thing as bringing a child into the family out of wedlock. Up until that point, I had dreams of attending Spelman College—the school that I want you and your sisters to attend. Kami, I want so much more for you," Mama said as she wiped the tears that were streaming from her eyes. I moved closer to her and wrapped my arms around her nuzzling up against her cheek as I had done when I was little.

So that's why she had always been so adamant with my sisters and me about where we would go to school. Her choice to have me and to marry my father had changed her life and cost her a dream. She wanted that dream for me, though.

Damien and I had really messed up. Our actions had thrown her a major curve ball.

Just then, Dad entered the room. Neither one of us had heard him come in. We had missed all of the pomp and circumstance that normally ensued when he entered. Usually,

my sisters would begin their chant, spelling out his name—
"D-A-D-D-Y." "D-A-D-D-Y."—and Mama and I were typically
right there with them to greet him with welcome home hugs
and kisses. Today was different, and he could tell.

"Why the heavy faces?" Daddy said.

Neither Mama nor I knew what to say. There was no denying that something was wrong.

Mama blurted out, "Kami is pregnant."

The expression on Daddy's face instantly changed from
happiness to terror.

"What?" he snapped. Daddy's face grew red and puffy as
his smile dropped "And let me guess by who. I'm going to kill
that little motherfucker. I never trusted him for an instant."
Daddy said as he ran to the closet in search of his forty-five.

Mama jumped up from the bed, cutting Daddy off just as
he got to the gun safe. She put her arms around him, and
motioned for me to exit the room.

I left without a second thought because I know what he
is like when he is angry. I have seen him erupt like a volcano before. It was going to take an act of congress to calm
him down and I didn't want to be anywhere around during
the process.

Behind me, I heard Mama spelling out every miserable
detail of the story to Daddy.

I didn't hear Daddy saying anything at all.

I waited.

The aged hardwood floors in our home creaked to alert
me that they were headed my way, down the long hallway that
separated my bedroom from theirs.

My heart pounded at a pace that made me fear it would
jump out of my chest. *What were they going to say to me? What*

was I going to do? Clearly, running away was not an option. There was only one way to enter my room, and only one way to exit. To get to the front door, I would have to pass them. I had no choice but to sit there and face the music. I had never felt so alone. Where was Damien now? It was his idea to go all the way.

I realized the meaning of the statement "Mama's baby, Daddy's maybe."

I could see the disappointment in my Mama and Daddy's faces as they stood in the doorway of my room. Daddy, a handsome brown-skinned man, looked defeated. Eyes puffy as if he had been crying. His face carried the wear of the news he had just received.

And Mama, who was light as ivory—her eyes were dark and piercing.

I had already prepared myself for the conversation, which was sure to be the worst experience of my life.

In a surprisingly calm voice, Daddy said, "There is no way that I am going to allow you to go through this alone. So pick up that phone, call Damien, and tell him that I expect him to be at this house within the hour."

I was in shock.

Daddy was asking me—actually, requiring me—to have Damien show up and take responsibility for his part in our actions.

I reached for the phone and dialed Damien's phone number.

He answered on the first ring. "Kami, are you ok? My God, I was terrified when I realized your Mama was on the phone listening to our conversation."

"Kami," Daddy said, his voice terse.

Nervous at the thought of making Daddy wait any longer, I said, "Damien, my Dad has asked that you come to our house, and he would like you to be here within the hour."

"Kami, I am supposed to be at Little Caesar's in an hour."

"Dad, Damien said that he has to be to work in an hour." I could hear my voice squeak with my terror.

In a voice loud enough for Damien and probably the entire street to hear, my Daddy said, "If that little nigger doesn't have his ass at my house within the hour, I am going to meet his ass at that damn job and see about him."

Damien said, "Please tell your father I'll be there within the next thirty minutes."

Without saying goodbye, Damien and I hung up.

Daddy stormed out of my room mumbling under his breath something to the effect of "How dare he test me, don't he know I'll kill his little ass?"

Mama, standing motionless at the edge of the bed, parted her lips to say something but decided against it, turned around, and followed Daddy up the hallway to the keeping room next to the kitchen.

For the next hour, we all awaited Damien's arrival. There was no activity in the house. I tried to calm my nerves as I waited in my room listening to my sisters' gleeful screams coming from the backyard as they played in their playhouse. The playhouse, which had been carefully fashioned after our home by our grandfather, was a true replica, down to the chamois paint and the rust shutters that flanked the windows.

I was so engrossed in thought about the care Grandpa had taken in building us a miniature version of our home, that I didn't hear the doorbell ring or Mama and Daddy calling me to join them up front. By the time I came to, Mama was at my doorway. "Didn't you hear your Daddy calling you?" Mama asked, slightly agitated.. "We've been calling your name for the past few minutes. Damien is here. Get up and come with me."

Damien was seated in the keeping room on one of our pink wingback chairs, still as a statue.

Daddy was in his big cream recliner, positioned diagonal to Damien. It was clear that everyone had been waiting on me.

Mama and I settled onto the pink striped loveseat and I braced myself for the fireworks.

"Damien, do you have any idea why I asked you here today," Daddy said.

"Yes sir, I believe I do." He glanced at me, then back at my Daddy. "There is a possibility that Kameleon is pregnant, sir."

"And how do you think we feel about that, Damien?" Daddy asked.

"Not good, sir."

"Why do you think we don't feel good about it, Damien?"

"Because we're so young?"

"Kami told us that she saw you put a condom on."

"Yes sir, I did."

"I'm going to ask you this question only once, young man, so I want you to really think about the answer you give me."

Damien began to squirm in his chair, as if he already knew the question that Daddy was about to ask him.

I grew increasingly uncomfortable by Damien's mannerisms. I couldn't imagine what Daddy was about to ask but it appeared that Damien did. "Did you keep the condom on, Damien? Meaning, did you take the condom off at any point?"

I looked at Daddy shocked by his question and then we all stared at Damien in anticipation of his response. The air was so thick a spatula could have cut it.

In a soft voice, Damien replied, "I did."

"You did what Damien?" Daddy asked for clarification.

"I took the condom off sir."

I gasped for air at the words, not sure what to do as Damien kept his eyes firmly planted on the floor in front of his feet.

"Damien, what do you mean?" I tried to fight back the tears that were pooling in my eyes. "I trusted you to protect us. I saw you put the condom on. Why did you take it off?"

"I wanted to see what you felt like without the condom. Before I knew it, I was cumming inside you. I couldn't stop. I'm sorry, Kami."

Daddy and Mama sat in silence as they listened in shock. In fact, we were all shocked to hear such graphic detail.

"How could you be so selfish? Did you even think about me? Did you even think about what I wanted? About my goals and dreams?" I asked through my sobs.

Mama put her arm around me.

Never had I felt so stupid and humiliated. I didn't know what to feel. My emotions were all over the place. One second, I was boiling with anger, like a teapot in full whistle. The next, I was hurt that someone I loved and trusted could deceive me so deeply.

For a moment, we all sat in the silence.

"Are you two ready to be parents?" Daddy asked.

"Sir, I am willing to take full responsibility for my actions. I love your daughter and would do anything for her. I knew that there was a risk of her getting pregnant when I took that condom off. I want her to have my child. I want us to be a family," Damien said.

"What about what I want, Damien?" I shouted. "Did you ever consider that I wasn't ready to be a mother? You didn't give me a choice. In fact, you took away my choice when you took off that condom." I slammed my hand on the coffee table knocking over Mama's three tiny angel figurines. "I had no idea you did that!" I exclaimed. "I have goals. I want to go to college and study law. I can't do that if I have a baby. Besides, how can I have a baby with you if I can't trust you?"

I turned to my father. "No, Daddy, I'm not ready to be a parent. I can't even take care of myself, let alone bring another life into the equation."

"Kami, our faith doesn't support abortion," Daddy said.

"I know, Daddy. But he deceived me. Shouldn't I have a say in whether or not I have a child?"

"Damien, are your parents aware of what's going on?" Daddy asked.

"Yes, sir. I told my father earlier today after Kami and I realized Mrs. Papillon was on the phone."

"Please call your father right now. We need to discuss our next steps. This situation not only impacts you and Kameleon, it involves our entire family. You two are minors, which means that we as parents are also responsible," Daddy said.

Mama, Damien, and I sat in silence as we listened to Daddy and Mr. Curry discuss the predicament Damien and I had gotten ourselves into. It was clear by Daddy's tone and responses that Mr. Curry believed that neither Damien nor I was ready to raise a child, and he felt that I should not be put through the embarrassment of a teenage pregnancy, especially one that had come about through deceit.

Mr. Curry said that he was in support of whatever decision our family made, and felt that ultimately I should be given a choice. He agreed to support our decision financially or as a grandparent.

As I listened, I gained a greater respect for both my father and Mr. Curry. They were standing with their children despite the situation. Although my respect for these two men was growing by the moment, I knew my perspective on men was changing. I had been introduced to the brutal side of sexuality before I'd had a chance to experience it as God had intended.

After Damien left that afternoon, I never spoke with him again—not because my parents forbade me, but because there was no purpose. I was no longer the trusting little girl blinded by faith and love and the hope of good will.

I was damaged goods, scared and untrusting, never to be the same.

SEPTEMBER 17, 1997

The elevator dinged open. I let out a deep cleansing breath and stepped out, happy to have some time alone. Christian and Carl would be together for the next couple of hours closing out the case.

I needed to pull it together before I saw Christian again, and definitely needed to calm down before I retrieved Ethan from Ms. Richards's house. I decided to swing by my parents' car lot, which was a mile away from the courthouse.

Upon entry, Mama nervously embraced me with a side hug and quickly ushered me to the back office where we could talk in private. I hated going back there and for the life of me never understood why my normally normal parents had junk all over the place. Why wouldn't she and Daddy clean up? There was stuff strewn all over the floor in a kind of a maze format. Mama glided through the mess with ease as she drug me along behind her. I had to watch my every step, otherwise I would have wound up on the ground, accosted by either the bucket filled with auto detail supplies by the door or the helium tank. Fortunately,

I barely missed the basketball goal that had been conveniently left in the middle of the floor.

"I'm dying to hear what happened in court today," Mama said with her deep brown eyes locked in on me like a target. Anxiously awaiting my response, she fidgeted with her hair finally tucking a few loose strands behind her right ear.

Daddy was finishing up a deal with a customer, so it would be a minute before he was able to join us. I only wanted to tell the awful story once.

"How was your day," I asked Mama to throw her off track from asking me about court.

She immediately went into her normal spiel about how busy they were and how much she wished Daddy would get them some help around the place. Everyone in the family knew the real story. Every time Daddy hired someone, Mama ran them off.

"We had an interesting visitor today," Mama said with a mischievous smile.

"You did? Really? Who?"

"Daddy and I debated whether or not to mention it to you, but we felt it wouldn't be right to keep it a secret."

I had already had enough excitement for one day, and I didn't have the strength to take any more. "Mama, spill it, please. I'm not in the mood to play a guessing game."

"Apparently," Mama said pausing for effect, "Lynie ran into William Levy at the mall recently." Mama scanned my face for any sign of interest as she continued to unveil her story. "She told him about our car lot, so he stopped by to say hello. Daddy and I both knew that he could care less about us and was really looking to dig up information on you." She touched her hair again re-securing the same strands that had somehow flown away again, then smugly grinned awaiting any sign of interest from me. I listened quietly with a blank stare making certain not to give her anything. The least ounce of interest I revealed would send her yacking to Auntie Mina about how she didn't know if Christian and I were going to make it because my college sweetheart was hunting me down. Even though I wondered the same, I didn't need anyone else in my ear trying to tell me what to do about my husband. My sisters and friends were enough. Mama proudly continued, "I was trying to be closed-lipped, but you know your big-mouth Daddy spilled it all. He told him where you worked and everything."

"Have mercy." I said in a flat disinterested tone. "I haven't seen or heard from William in years."

My mother yacked on, as I reflected and smiled inwardly. I wondered what in the world William was doing coming to my parents' car lot. The last time I heard from him was the week before Christian and I married.

William and I had been a serious item off and on through-out our college years, and had been through a lot together, so we were *close*. When he couldn't afford to go home for break, he stayed at our house—on the couch, no less, but at our house. He was the first guy my parents allowed to stay in our home. He was even at our home when he got his NFL draft call. Everyone in our families thought for sure we would end up together.

But events change us. After he was drafted, things got really crazy. Women were everywhere, money was flowing, and our relationship became more than we could handle.

I was still in college, but he had graduated and begun his professional football career. We finally broke it off for good after I entered his hotel room only to find another woman there with him. Why would he give me a key to a hotel room where he knew he would be inviting other women? Was it some sick fetish of his where he wanted me to walk in on him and catch him in the company of another woman? He was so young and full of himself, flying high on top of the world. It was definitely in my best interest to just move on before he hurt me any further, so I did just that.

The next time I spoke with him was when he called the week before my wedding to ask me if I was sure I wanted to marry Christian. The nerve of this guy. Apparently, one of his boys had seen our marriage announcement and told him. I remember asking him, "Why are you calling me?" Then following up with, "You know that you're not even concerned or close to settling down. Is this an entertaining exercise for you or something?"

Daddy interrupted my random wonderings as he entered the back office area announcing his presence by tripping over the tricycle I barely managed to miss. As he collected himself and made his way over to Mama and me, he had the nerve to mumble, "I don't know why someone won't clean up around here." We all chuckled.

"So, how did things go in court today?" Dad asked.

"It was really intense, Daddy. I lost my cool," I replied.

"What do you mean? That judge didn't deport that woman?" Mama asked.

"Yes, Mama. The judge extended my protection order, cleared Christian of the charges, and decided to send her back to Somalia. The thing that got under my skin was, as they were taking her away to the holding room, she had the nerve to look me in my eyes and say, with a smirk, 'Kami, I may be gone physically, but a part of me will always be with Christian.'

I could feel my face getting hot again, just recounting it for them. "Before I could contain myself, I blurted out, 'Bitch, you were just a jump-off for when I wasn't around. You didn't know your place.'"

"Kami I can't believe you said that." Mama exclaimed as Daddy looked on, studying my face. "I taught you better than that. You can never stoop to her level. You're a lady and should always act as such. This whole mess is beginning to take you outside of yourself all the cussing and carrying on."

Dad and I both gave her a blank stare that caused her to quickly stifle her rant.

Mama was all about decorum and her girls presenting themselves in a polished, pulled-together light no matter what was going on. We could be crumbling inside or about to combust, but we better damn well look and sound good.

"Avery, let the girl finish," Daddy said.

After a few moments of silence, he realized I had no more words, and asked, "Do you have any idea what she meant by being gone physically, but that part of her would always be with Christian."

Until that moment, I hadn't thought about any kind of meaning to her words.

"I have no idea, Daddy, but I'm certain I'll find out. It seems I always do, whether I want to or not."

AUGUST 18, 1990

It was Freshman Week in the Atlanta University Center. All the recruits for Spelman, Morehouse, Clark Atlanta University, and Morris Brown had been called in a week early to be shown the ropes before the semester began. Along with ten other girls, I was temporarily housed in the basement of Howard Harold, and I was less than excited.

Although Spelman is a premier women's institution, the housing department clearly did not have their shit together because they had yet to release the rooms from the young ladies who had decided not to attend this fall. As a result, we were forced to live in sub-par accommodations that mirrored those of the orphanage in the Broadway show *Annie.*

As you can imagine, this did not bode well with most of us. Almost every girl at Spelman had come from a privileged background, where they had enjoyed luxuries like personal space. I had never in my life shared a room with anyone, and now, at the age of seventeen, I was sharing a room with ten other girls I'd never met.

It worried me. I had never gotten along with girls. In fact, every girl I'd ever gone to school with had made it a point to make my life a living hell. My room, personal time, and space was my refuge, and I had none of those at this moment. I had been excited about entering the next phase of my life up until this point. Now, I felt like I had taken a step back into the dark years instead of moving forward.

There was no air conditioning in the older dorms on Spelman's campus, and Howard Harold was no exception. "It's hot as Hades in here." Mama said as she wiped the sweat that was quickly forming on her brow. "Spelman ought to be ashamed of themselves," she said with a look of disgust. "Don't they realize it's August and we are in the damn South?"

Daddy continued in an audible mumbled, "Got us paying all this goddam money and our daughter is on a cot in a basement with no air."

I looked around the basement. The walls were dark, damp, and dingy, and the windows were formed by three narrow horizontal slits. "These are prison windows," I said.

"No baby, the windows in prison are larger than those." Daddy frowned at the window nearest him.

Mama, my sisters and I frowned as we surveyed our surroundings.

The blinds on the windows were drawn tightly closed. No one could see in, and we definitely could not see out. Even when I tried to open the tiny blinds to let a little light in, it didn't help, so the only light in the room came from two rusted light fixtures hanging from the ceiling on equally rusted chains. They looked as though they had literally been there for as long as the building, so it wouldn't have surprised me one bit if one hit the dust.

Cots were lined up to face each other along each wall.

I chose one of the two cots that had been positioned diagonally apart from the others. Because of the shock and awe the facilities provided, I was in full cry, and every time Mama unpacked something, I tried to put it back into the box. I didn't even realize another girl and her parents had entered the dungeon. She blurted out through her tears, "Oh, no, I can't stay here."

Her parents tried to console her while claiming the other cot that was apart from the group, on a diagonal from me. Meanwhile, the girl was sitting on top of her suitcase, refusing to move.

We were both sobbing about being left in the hellhole.

Noticing Mama and I were in the same emotional space dealing with this mess, the lady walked over with her daughter in her arms.

"Hi, I'm Kat, and this is my daughter Moni. Is this a mess or what," the other girl's mother said.

Were we going to be friends or foes, I wondered. In my past, by no fault of my own, I'd had enough enemies. If she was going to be added to the collection, then it was not going to be my fault. I tried to grin, and she returned a smile.

"Mess is an understatement. I'm Avery, and this is my daughter Kami Papillon."

Moni and I looked at each other through tears and smudged eye makeup, sizing each other up.

"Papillon. Isn't that French?" Moni asked, voice still cracking from her tears.

"Yes, it means butterfly." I quietly responded.

Moni was a petite girl, standing all of five feet tall with long silky black hair and an olive complexion. Her eyes were slanted and her features looked Asian, even though her mother and father clearly were not.

"Mr. and Mrs. Papillon," a tiny voice squealed breaking the standoff between Moni and I. We all turned around, trying to figure out who was calling my parents' names, and who could possibly be this excited about being in temporary housing hell.

"Anya," I squealed, jumping up from the cot. "I haven't seen you since seventh grade graduation. Oh my God, how have you been? Are you coming here this Fall?"

"I am," Anya gleefully replied as she tightly hugged my neck.

Anya and I had been best buds in elementary school. I'd often played mother hen for her on picture day and most special occasions because her hair was always all over her head, a mess on the best of days.

"Who knew we would end up at the same college?" I said as I tightly hugged her back.

"Hey Moni." Anya said.

"Wait, you two know each other?" I asked.

"Yes. We went to high school together." Anya replied.

Anya hugged my neck tight and turned to Moni. "This here is my girl. She took good care of me when we were in elementary school. For some reason, on picture day, I could never keep it together. When it was time for me to take my picture, the hair right here in the front of my head formed a halo and always showed up as naps when our proofs came back. Thank God Kami always carried a brush."

We all giggled, including our parents. Anya had definitely lightened up the atmosphere, as she always had.

The basement room quickly filled with other girls from all over the country who looked like us and came from families like ours. I began to relax as Anya and Moni introduced me to Alexa and Bella, who had also attended high school with them. In less than twenty minutes, I had made more friends than I had in my entire high school career. There was no pretense, because we were all on a level playing field. We were all beautiful, smart, and had a lot going for us—and, on top of that, we had so much in common. We were so busy chatting it up that none of us noticed our parents leave.

That afternoon, Anya, Moni, Alexa, Bella, and I formed a sisterhood. We quickly took turns helping each other unpack and get settled into our holding space. Not receiving a room assignment was turning out to be okay, sweaty walls and all. Maybe temporary housing wasn't going to be so bad.

AUGUST 23, 1990

"Rise and shine," Anya screamed as she entered the room.

I took the pillow and covered my head trying to drown out her shrieks while Moni screamed, "Enough already."

Anya was dressed and ready to roll while Moni and I were trying to get just a few more seconds of sleep before the day began.

"Come on you guys," Anya said. "Freshman convocation starts in 15 minutes. We have to make it on time or we will get more demerits."

We had made it to Thursday and freshman week was finally winding down. In the process however, our little crew had been racking up demerits all week for being late to mandatory activities. There had been so many; the brother sister tea, orientation, opening convocation, and the list went on and on. It was a lot to get use to all at one time. However, if we were late to convocation today, we would not be able to attend the scrimmage at noon and that was not an option.

"Nobody told you two to stay out all night. Now look at you," Anya said through a giggle.

She was right. We should have come in with her last night but instead; I stayed with Moni who had glued herself to a cutie named Corey. I didn't want to leave her alone with him and his friends. Hell, we didn't know them. Now, we had all of 10 minutes to get into our white dresses, flesh tone stockings and black shoes. It would take at least five minutes to walk to Sister's Chapel on the other side of campus.

Realizing what was in jeopardy, Moni and I quickly kicked it into high gear managing to peel ourselves off our cots, get dressed, and make it to Sister's Chapel in record time securing our attendance to the scrimmage just before they bolted the doors.

"This is like an all you can eat buffet," Bella announced mesmerized by the sea of people and handsome men that unfolded before our eyes as we entered the scrimmage. "Clearly everyone who is anyone is here," Alexa added flipping her hair and placing her hand on her right hip. Moni and I made a b-line to the concession stand for cold drinks while Alexa, Bella and Anya went to secure a spot in the stands. As we waited in line, Corey and his lame crew walked up. "Hey ladies," Corey said with a huge cheesy grin on his face. Blushing Moni said, "Hi Corey." I wasn't about to get caught up babysitting Moni and Corey again so I said, "Moni, I'm going to go see if I can find the girls, I will send Alexa back to help with the drinks." "Ok girl, Moni said and then turned back to her conversation with Corey. Just as I was turning to walk away I saw him. I don't know whether it was the mystery in his eyes or the firmness of his ass that got me first, but whatever the case, I was completely mesmerized.

Isn't it amazing that women share the same desires as men? We are subtler with our shit, but the desires are the same. We don't yell out stuff like "Hey sexy" or "Hey shawty, can I get a little trim?" *What the hell is trim anyway?*

Instead, we want to know what's in their heads and pockets before we get to know what's between their legs. Have some casual conversation, maybe a movie, dinner, something of more substance before we give up the ass.

But anyway, there I was, just standing there undressing this man, and he hadn't even looked my way. *He'd be fun to play with.* Call it what you might, but a woman has needs too. I had to get his attention.

I sauntered toward him and strategically placed my body in a location where he was sure to see me. Anya and Bella walked up. "What's taking you and Moni so long?" Bella asked.

"Shh. Look at that," I said as I discreetly pointed in the guy's direction. Anya and Bella looked in the direction of my finger and their mouths' dropped open.

"That's William. He is the star running back at GA Tech we were talking about the other night." Anya said. "You didn't mention he looked like that," I whispered through clenched teeth as I stared and William moved closer. "Watch this girls," I said with a devious smirk. As he approached, I positioned myself so that he was sure to brush my round derriere as he passed. I glanced back at my girls to make sure they were still looking and mouthed "Take notes." They giggled in the background anxiously awaiting the *meeting*. I was perched, composed, and confident – waiting because I just knew he was going to say something me, and do you know that nigga said "Excuse me," and walked around me like I was a stone pillar.

I thought I was going to pass out and die. "I'm taking notes alright. Taking notes on what not to do," Bella yelled out as her and Anya fell out laughing.

In utter shock, I mumbled, "Oh no he didn't just pass by me as I was perched up here waiting on him to say something to me." Anya and Bella continued to laugh hysterically until I cut my eyes at them. They stopped laughing.

"I'm not going to be defeated," I told them.

I walked over to him and noticed a smirk on his face.

He swirled around and began walking toward me. As he approached, he said, "It takes a little more than a round ass to get my attention. I would much rather look at your beautiful face. I'm William. And you are…" he asked as he extended his hand to shake mine.

My girls and his boys surrounded us rolling laughing as I stood in front of him in shock. I didn't see a damn thing funny because I knew he was going to be a challenge.

AUGUST 26, 1990

Peeks of blue and orange darted across the waning night sky signaling daybreak as Moni, Anya and I tip toed out of the beer bash we had entered 5 hours before. The music was still blaring as Corey and his boys milled around cleaning up and preparing to host a cookout and part two of what they had begun yesterday. Although his friends were lame, our crew had cosigned on Corey for Moni. He was a really nice guy and one of the only freshman that had his own house near campus. "Where are you three sneaking off to?" Corey yelled. "Kami has to meet her parents at church and Anya and I need to go get cleaned up," Moni responded. "Y'all are coming back later right? It was yawl's idea to cookout today," Corey said with furrowed brow. "Relax Corey. We are coming back," Moni said. You need anything from the store?"

"Naw, I think we are straight but call me before you head back over in case we need some last minute items. Moni kissed him on the forehead and we dashed out the front door. I barely had time to brush my teeth and drop them at the dorm before I met my family for early morning mass. As usual, I was late, and rocking the same clothes from the night before, but I was there. The going joke with my friends was that no matter how late I partied, there were two places I was going to be. I was going to make it to work and I was going to church.

Sometimes I think my Mama secretly wished that I would just miss church. All of her friends made it a point to speak to me on those days when I dragged in after clubbing all night, just to see Mama squirm.

After church, we had brunch at Chantrelle's, a soul food restaurant close to campus. Sunday brunch with the family was everything to me. After eating in the dining hall all week long I welcomed a good meal. My friends would always flock to me to see what leftovers I had when we return from church and I happily shared, always ordering enough so that everyone could have a little taste.

"Another long night I see," Mama said as she eyed me from the side and placed a fork full of macaroni and cheese in her mouth at the same time.

I knew it was coming so I took in a deep breath and braced myself.

"Kami you could at least change clothes. Coming into the Lord's house smelling like alcohol and smoke. Church is a sacred place child."

Mama paused long enough for me to let out an audible mumble. "The Lord said come as you are."

"Don't sass me child. I know what the Lord says but I'm telling you that sometimes I wish you would miss early Mass and take the time to get yourself together. My friends have a field day on me about you every Sunday" Mama said pushing her plate away in disgust.

"Your friends are snobs and by the way, where are their children? At least I still come to church."

"Now now you two," Daddy chimed in signaling he had heard enough and we were now disturbing his meal."

"I apologize for being such an embarrassment." I said softly after taking stock of my attire. Cut-off shorts, really? I did look a mess and was definitely ready for a shower.

"Kami, I can't believe it's been nearly two weeks and you're still in temporary housing. Any word on your room assignment?" Mama asked as we headed back to campus. "No Mama. Not a word."

"We are paying over twenty thousand dollars a year for you to attend Spelman and to live on campus. It is unacceptable that you are still in that basement," Daddy said. "I am beginning to get very agitated. If I was two weeks late with your tuition I bet I would be hearing something from them," Daddy continued with a frown indicating he was bothered. Daddy hardly ever frowned.

"Daddy please don't go up in there cussing and making a scene. I have to deal with these people for the next four years."

"When have you known us to make a scene Kami?" Mama interjected. "We are not leaving this campus today without talking to someone in housing and that is that." Mama concluded.

Before heading over to the housing department, we stopped by my temporary digs to put my leftovers in the mini refrigerator Mama and I had managed to smuggle in by my cot. There was a note on my bed.

"What is it," Mama said.

"I need to report to the housing department." I ran over and hugged my mom. "I've been assigned a room."

"Oh Kami. That is great news. Let's go out and tell your Daddy before he flips a gasket." Mama and I ran out to the car to tell Daddy the good news.

"Daddy, I got my room assignment." I yelled before I could get to the car good. "I guess God knew best because Lord knows I was about to show out" Daddy said.

We all laughed as Daddy put the hazard lights on and hopped out of the car with my sisters.

"We will stay here and start packing and loading your things in the car while you and Mama go to the housing department to get your room keys. Avery, when you find out what dorm she has been assigned to, call the basement pay phone and let me know and the girls and I will meet you two over there."

"Thanks Daddy, I said as I kissed him on the forehead and darted to the housing department with Mama in tow.

"I am thrilled that I won't have to sleep on a cot tonight and I finally have the opportunity to have a real college experience with a roommate."

"Me too honey. Now, if I can just get you to go home at night instead of partying till dawn, we will really be doing something," Mama said with a smirk.

"Thank goodness I did meet you all at church," I said. "I surely need all of you to help me gather my things and get moved in."

Mama gave me a blank stare and then we both broke out into laughter.

"I am happy that we went ahead and got all of the shopping out of the way. You have your comforter, sheets and all kinds of things to organize your space and make it feel like your home away from home." Mama continued.

A fleeting moment of sadness swooped in as I thought this is now my home away from home. I was entering into a new chapter of my life. *I was finally out of Mama's house and didn't know whether to be excited or afraid.* In a melancholy tone I replied, "Yea, today is the perfect day for this to happen." Sensing my hesitation, Mama glanced at me and softly touched my cheek turning my face toward hers.

"I am so very proud of you Kami. You're about to do something that Mama wished she could have done. I want you to do your best baby girl and most of all, have fun." Smiling she continued, "Daddy and I are only 20 minutes away. If you need us, we will come running. I promise."

As we approached the Living and Learning Center Two, the building in which the housing department was located, we spotted a pegboard with several lists attached. Mama and I searched the lists for my name amongst all of the room assignments and finally located it in the section for Packard Hall.

"Go figure, I would be assigned to Packard Hall; *the dorm that started it all and only the oldest building on campus.*" I remarked sarcastically.

"How historic Kami, you get to stay in the first building erected on campus. This is just so special baby." As far as Mama was concerned, Spelman could do no wrong.

"Yea Mama, so special. Packard is older than Howard Harold," I said with a slight frown. "If Howard Harold has no air conditioning, I am sure Packard doesn't.

"Stop acting spoiled." Mama snapped. "There are millions of people in this world who survive every day without air conditioning. Surely you can as well," Mama concluded in a huff as she dropped her quarter in the pay phone to call

Daddy over in Howard Harold to let him know I had been assigned to Packard and we were headed over.

I could surmise from bits and pieces of the conversation that Daddy and my sisters were almost finished packing and loading my things and would be heading our way in five minutes.

Mama got off the phone we headed over to Packard.

"Lord have mercy," Mama said fanning herself as we walked through the doors of Packard. "I take everything I said to you back honey, it is hot as hell in here."

I glanced at Mama with a blank stare and said nothing.

"This isn't any better than the basement," she said, looking around.

In the foyer was a young lady sitting at a desk behind a glass window. I showed her the note I'd received in the housing department, and she handed me an ID card, and two antique keys. "This key opens the front door of the building and this is your room key. Follow me," she said without a smile.

We proceeded into the vast lobby. The ancient wood walls donned pictures that outlined the history of the illustrious all women's institution. Large oil paintings of Sophia Packard and Harriet Giles, Spelman's founders and the Rockefellers were prominently hung acknowledging the family as Spelman's benefactors. The mahogany floors were covered with faded tapestry rugs that had anchored the steps of so many who had come before me. Though worn and aged, there was something majestic about the structure that kept you from complaining and being self-absorbed; something that humbled you and made you appreciative of being in her recesses.

We made a right entering into a long hallway lined on each side with enormous wooden doors each with a room number posted in the center on a large brass plate. We proceeded all the way to the end of the hallway stopping before the last large wooden door on the right hand side.

There was a welcome sign posted on the outside of the door that read Kirby and Shanice. "Here is your room," the insipid young lady announced. "Our first dorm meeting is this evening at 6 p.m. Please be on time."

With that she departed leaving Mama and I standing outside of the door.

We could hear a voice mumbling inside. I knocked, and we waited a minute.

"Perhaps she's on the phone and can't hear us knocking," Mama said.

I turned the key in the lock and pushed open the heavy wooden door. Mama and I walked inside.

The room was configured like one of those "shot gun" houses back in the day, long and narrow. Each side of the room had a desk and a twin bed. There was one window in the center of the back wall and in front of the window stood a young lady who was about five feet seven inches tall, at least a good four inches taller than me. She was on the phone, which explained the mumbling Mama and I had heard from outside of the door.

"But Shanice, you're my best friend, we promised each other that we were both coming to Spelman and we were going to be roommates. What do you mean you aren't coming? Why didn't you tell me that before I left? You're really leaving me to the wolves," Kirby concluded before she turned to look at Mama and me.

Just then, Daddy and my sisters filed in loaded down with my things. Dia handed me my purple Caboodle and then went to help stack my other things on the twin bed located on the right side of the room since Kirby alreadyoccupied the left side of the room.

Kirby stood looking at my family, all my things, and me with her mouth open ear still plastered to the phone. We were all crammed into the tiny room. She didn't say anything to us. She just looked at us, from one to the other. Then she turned back toward the window and whispered into the phone, "I have to go. Whitley just walked in."

Whitley was the snooty character from the popular 1980's college sitcom *A Different World*. Those who watched the show either loved Whitley or hated her. She came from a privileged southern family and couldn't relate to the plight of those less fortunate.

I was offended. This chick didn't even know me. Every young lady I'd met so far had been amazing and I'd connected with them. Was this some kind of cruel joke? Why did my roommate have to be a *mean girl*? Her rudeness had taken me completely by surprise. I was lost for words. In order to break the ice, Mama said, "Hi, I'm Mrs. Papillon and this is my daughter Kameleon. You two are going to be roommates this year. This is my husband and these two are Dia and Lynie."

"I'm Kirby," the girl said flatly.

I felt like I was back in high school. My sisters and I began to unpack my things while Mama and Daddy went back out to the car for the final load.

Kirby tried to make casual conversation with me.

"Where are you from?" Kirby asked, fingering one of my sweaters. "What high school did you go to?"

I remained silent trying to decide if I wanted to answer Kirby or not.

"She is from here and went to Southwest DeKalb High School," Dia responded on my behalf. Once you cross me, it's hard to get back in my good graces. I had been around girls like Kirby my entire life and I wasn't trying to have one of *those* for my roommate. I carefully watched her movements, observing how she was trying to redeem herself by making room in the closet and helping me to get settled. My sisters and Mama seemed to be warming up to her which made me feel a little better.

After we finished hanging my pictures, making my bed, and getting my clothes into my side of the tiny closet, we were all pooped. What had started out as a typical Sunday had turned into an all-day affair. My family kissed me, said their goodbyes to Kirby and me, and headed home. As they walked out, Moni walked in.

"I can't believe this. You're in Packard too."

"Yes, and still no air conditioning. How are we going to make it?"

"Moni, this is my roommate Kirby. I think we are going to be ok as long as she refrains from calling me Whitley," I said with a smirk.

"Hi Moni," Kirby said her face flushed from embarrassment.

"Are we still going to Corey's this evening," I asked.

"Yea girl after the meeting," Moni replied

At the dorm meeting, we found out that Anya and the rest of the crew had also been assigned to Packard. My evening was getting better and better. Although Kirby went with Moni and me to the dorm meeting, I wasn't sure whether or not I was going to allow her into the fold of my new friends, especially since she made that comment about me.

However, Anya, as sweet as she is, knew no enemies, and graciously invited Kirby to part two of the beer bash we were planning to attend that evening.

Kirby was ecstatic and agreed to go. Before we left the room Kirby said, "I want to apologize to you for what I said earlier today. When you walked in, you had your Caboodle in your hand with your matching comforter and all this stuff. I was terrified that I was getting a roommate that was snooty and out of touch with reality. I understand if you don't want me to go with you and your friends tonight." Kirby was trying to apologize and make things right.

I could either forgive her or be a mean girl myself. "Girl, don't worry about it," I said.

"Let's go party."

SEPTEMBER 19, 1997

The Friday dismissal bell shrieked loudly marking the beginning of the weekend. Every child in my class—even sweet little Nicole—jumped up and ran out of the classroom before I could even part my lips to tell them that the bell does not dismiss them, I do. "Sit down and wait to be dismissed," I said to their backs as the door slammed behind them.

Despite my threats and admonishments, they still hadn't learned. **It had been a long horrific week.**

Christian was traveling for "work" and Ethan was spending the weekend with his Nana, so I was looking forward to having some time alone and the house to myself.

I had to complete my lesson plans for next week for my English classes, and get some order in my classroom before my weekend could start. My rambunctious eighth graders had wrecked my little haven of learning. "You guys are going to get it next week for leaving this mess," I said aloud. Balled-up paper was all over the floor, and someone had spilled an entire bag of chips. *Who the hell had chips in class?*

I was slipping. The events of the past few weeks and the court date were all taking a toll on me.

The intercom buzzed. "Ms. Papillon-Beck."

"Yes, Ms. Thomas?"

"You have a visitor in the front office."

"Okay, thanks, I'll be right up."

I tried to figure out who in the world could be visiting me at school at the end of the day on Friday. I rarely had any visitors, and I knew I had not scheduled any parent conferences. Mama and Daddy were at the car lot, my sisters were away at school, and Ethan was with his Nana. *Who could possibly be coming to see me?*

I straightened out my cardigan and adjusted my leather skirt, grateful that I had taken my time getting dressed, for the first time in weeks of depression and anxiety.

A figure stood in the foyer of the school, backlit and silhouetted. Close by a group of my female colleagues stood chatting, giggling and admiring the stranger. The closer I got, the better I could make out the face. It was William. *I should have known.* Mama told me that Daddy had told him where I worked, and I'd known it was only a matter of time before he would contact me. I never imagined that he would be bold enough to just show up at the school.

Everyone at the school knew I was married, and they knew this wasn't Christian. *How the hell was I going to play this off?* My colleagues knew he was not a parent at the school because we knew all of the dads, and none of them garnered this kind of attention.

"Kami Kam. What's going on, girl?" William said in his sexy raspy voice as he welcomed me with outstretched arms and a huge smile.

It had been so long since we had seen each other, but because of our audience, I couldn't look too happy. As I hugged him, I whispered, "You're my cousin."

No sooner had he released me than Ms. Smith hollered out, "Who is this specimen, Mrs. Papillon-Beck?"

I hollered back, trying to do a little damage control. "It's just my cousin William, ladies, pipe down." The ladies continued to oh, ah, and cackle as I giggled and William and I walked briskly down the hallway toward my classroom.

Once in the room, William asked, "What happened in here? Looks like a tornado hit. Need some help?"

"I will gladly accept your help," I said.

I erased the board as William returned the desks to their quads and swept up all the trash the children had left behind. As we cleaned, we made small talk, reminiscing and laughing about the day we met and our college years. Before too long, the room was back to normal.

"Why are you here," I asked as I took a seat in one of the freshly cleaned student desks and looked up at William. "You and I both know you didn't stop by on a Friday afternoon just to help me clean my classroom."

"I ran into your sister at the mall and I just couldn't get you off my mind. I had to see you, so I went by the car lot and saw Mom and Dad, and you know your Daddy, he ain't never been short on words." William perched on my desk. "He told me where you worked. I debated on whether or not I should come by. But something kept pulling me here. Pulling me towards you. So, I made up my mind that today I was coming to see you."

"What have you been up to? You still playing ball?"

"No, I retired about a year ago and settled back here in Atlanta. My wife…"

"Oh, your wife, huh?"

"Yes, my wife."

"Who did you end up marrying?" I asked with a smirk. "I thought you would never settle down."

"Michelle."

"I should have known. The big booty girl I caught you in the hotel room with."

"Yeah" William stuttered.

"I always did wonder what happened to her. I knew you had dated her before, and I was suspicious that you might have been dating her while we were together."

"Kami, Michelle and I were not together while you and I were dating. It is true that we were together before you and me, but I swear never while we were together."

"Uh huh," I said with a chuckle

"Anyway, you're the one who started this marriage thing. You got married first. I tried to call you to find out whether or not that was really what you wanted to do."

"William, you called me the week of my wedding. What in the world was I supposed to do with that? And, on top of that, you knew, you absolutely knew you were not ready to get married."

"Kami, you weren't ready to get married either. You and I both know the reason you married Christian was because you were looking for a way out. You were tired of living with your Mama and Daddy. You and your mother never got along, and you knew that the best way to get from under her rule was to move out of her house. After graduating, with student loans and grad school hanging over your head, you weren't in the position to live on your own. So you decided to marry Christian."

"William. How dare you. I loved Christian. I still love Christian."

"Hmmm, I heard some things about Christian in the streets, and then when I ran into Lynie, she shared with me that you could really use a friend right now. It's part of the reason why I wanted to come and check on you, to see how things were going."

"That damned Lynie. She has such a big mouth. She always did like you. I can count on her to keep everybody informed about all that is going on in my life. Geez."

"Don't be mad at your sister, Kami. She's just worried about you, that's all. I couldn't get you off my mind. You're married and I'm married. We both have a whole lot to lose, but there's nothing wrong with a little kindness and friendship. I'm going to leave my number, and if you decide that you want to meet me for dinner or drinks or whatever the case may be, call me. I'd love to hang out with you and catch up."

"I'll do just that, William."

With that, he opened his arms, hugged me tight, kissed me on the forehead, and walked out of the classroom. My crazy self, I couldn't get to the window fast enough to see what this fool was driving. He always had a taste for beautiful women and expensive cars. Low and behold, it was a brand new, black, big-body Benz. How interesting.

I thought about it. Maybe I would have coffee with him.

NOVEMBER 2, 1990

His penis thrust in and out of my mouth with such force I could feel it pounding into the back of my throat.

I had grown to like the carnal sensation of giving head and tasting the ejaculate as it oozed into my mouth. No longer was I the victim, the timid little girl that believed what men said. They all had a purpose, and I used them as players in my game and I discarded them when they no longer served my purpose.

For some reason, I was a music industry and football player magnet. I never searched them out, but they always found me. From my senior year in high school up until now, I had dated some of the top talents in the country, and found that all of them were easily controlled and manipulated by one thing. Sex. Sex was freedom. Sex was control. Sex got me anything I wanted, and I was good at it. The key was not to get caught up and never to allow them close enough to hurt you.

"Ughhh," William moaned as his sweet essence projected down my throat.

I had not intended to swallow, but the force of his ejaculation caught me off guard. As I released him gently from my mouth, his body collapsed onto the bed. I lay next to him with a smug look on my face. I knew he was mine and I could have anything I wanted from him.

"Your lips could start World War III," William said as he reached over in an attempt to cuddle with me. I quickly diverted his efforts.

I had learned that cuddling was a surefire way to get caught up. Cuddling was what caused people to catch feelings, and I definitely was not about the feelings. Once you catch feelings, it is hard to reel them in—and before you know it, you're sitting outside of someone's house like the Feds.

"What's up with that, Kami? Why won't you let me hold you? Why won't you let me in?" William snapped.

"I don't do that, William. Anyhow, what's a big ol' guy like you doing catching feelings? Stop that." We giggled, but I could tell William was still bothered by my diversion and was not about to let it go that easily.

"I do have feelings for you, Kami."

"Who are you trying to fool? All those women that hover around after your games to talk to you, do you really expect me to believe that you have feelings for little ol' me?"

"I do have feelings for little ol' you, and it's not just about the head. Although I must say you do give exceptional head."

I turned to smack William but he caught my hand just before it landed, and then leaned in and gave me a big, fat, sloppy kiss on the lips. His lips were full and they tasted and smelled like sex. I didn't mind. It was all love.

The sun was shining bright outside. I glanced over at the clock and realized I had two hours before I had to be at work. I jumped out of bed and rushed around the room, looking for my panties and gathering the rest of my clothes. I hadn't planned on spending the night with William, so now I had to rush back to my dorm, get showered and changed, and be on the other side of town by ten, when the car dealership opened. I was the weekend receptionist at my uncle's Lincoln Mercury store and no matter how much I partied I was focused. I always did my schoolwork, kept a steady part-time job, and made it to early mass on Sundays.

"Why are you in such a tizzy, Kami? It's eight o'clock on a Saturday morning."

"I have to get to work. Some of us don't have a full ride to school and boosters lining our pockets."

William cut his eyes at me and I pretended to cower away in fear. "Will I see you later at the game?" he asked.

"You bet. I get off at six and will be there with bells and whistles." I kissed him softly on the forehead and ran out the door to face my walk of shame back at the dorm.

SEPTEMBER 20, 1997

For the first morning in months, I woke up naturally. I didn't have to worry about Ethan taking his latest superhero toy and banging me upside my head saying, "Eat eat, Mommy, eat eat." I was free to go about my day at leisure, and had decided to treat myself to a spa day—massage, facial, mani, pedi, brows, and all the trimmings. My eyebrows were a hot mess and hadn't been groomed in months, so today was going to be all about me.

As I drew my bath water, I couldn't help thinking about the visitor I'd had at school the day before.

William still looked good. The same muscular build, strong jawline, and booming body he'd had in college with the same sex appeal. The only thing different was that in college he'd had a head full of sandy brown curly hair, but now he rocked a bald head. His body was clearly his temple, and you could tell he had spent his life maintaining it.

As I sank into my hot bath, I thought about my drooling colleagues and knew I was going to return to school with a million questions about my so-called "cousin." I couldn't do any better than that on the fly? Geez.

Why was this happening? Why was William drawn to me? Why did he feel the need to reach out? I am married. He is married. I have a kid. He has two kids. Neither of us are the same as we were in college. The footloose and fancy-free beauty who did anything she wanted and dared anyone to question her was no more. In her place stood a woman that had been worn by the experiences of life. I have to say that his timing was impeccable, though. I chuckled at that thought because if ever there was a time that I was weak, it was right now. Who was I kidding? No matter how badly Christian treated me, I was committed to our relationship. Committed to the vows we'd made on August 19, 1995. But, I was curious. Did I still have the ability to make men succumb to my every desire? Back then, I'd used sex, shopping, alcohol and men to bury my pain from a lack of acceptance and loneliness I'd experienced throughout my childhood and teenage years.

After all the shit I had been through over the past few months, seeing William had awakened something in me that I had buried when I decided to marry. Pandora 's Box was open and all kinds of thoughts were racing through my mind as I drove to Spa Sydell. I was hurting and I wanted Christian to feel the pain I was feeling. I wanted him to hurt too.

Did I still have it?

As I exited the spa I felt refreshed. It was almost as if Zena was able to sense the tension in my body through osmosis because she zeroed right in on the spots that were most tense and needed release. It was always the center of my upper back and my hips around my sciatic nerve. As I walked to my car I remembered that today was the day before Lynie's birthday and since I had time to spare. I decided to call her when I got settled inside of my car to ask if she wanted to meet me for lunch.

The first time I called the phone went to voicemail but the second time she picked up immediately. "Hey sissy. What's up?"

"Hey sissy. I was wondering if you wanted to meet me for lunch. I know tomorrow is your birthday and I was hoping to treat you to a little something special. We hardly ever get the opportunity to spend time with each other with me working so much lately and you finishing up school."

"That would be great," Lynie said. "Where would you like me to meet you?" she asked.

"Well I'm just leaving Spa Sydell in Buckhead. Brio is right up the street. We can meet there for lunch and cocktails if you like?"

"Brio's is perfect. I'm on my way."

I hung up the phone, started the car, and began to drive toward Brio. It was so beautiful outside. Not a cloud in the sky. I decided to drop the top on my car and take in the sun of the clear crisp day. It was rare that I had the opportunity to put the top back on my silver convertible BMW 325i because the pollen count in Atlanta was off the charts. Something was always blooming and I was allergic to almost everything. Today, Mother Nature had given us a reprieve and I intended to enjoy every minute of it.

I arrived first, tossed my keys to the valet, and walk inside the restaurant. For some reason, I was feeling myself today. It had been a long time since I felt this good. I'm not sure if it was the spa treatments or the fact that I was going to spend some time with my sissy but whatever it was my energy was on 10.

I decided to take a seat on the patio, which made for the perfect place to see and be seen. I loved to people watch so this location would provide ample entertainment while I waited on Lynie to arrive.

A bubbly young lady approached the table and said, "Welcome to Brio ma'am. My name is Ashley and I will be your server today. Are you expecting other guests?"

"Yes, Ashley, I am waiting on my sister to arrive. Her birthday is tomorrow and I decided to treat her to cocktails and lunch. Do you offer anything special for those who celebrate their birthdays with you?"

"Yes ma'am we will make sure that she gets a little something from Brio to celebrate her special day. While you wait, may I offer you a beverage?"

"Yes. What kind of champagne do you have by the glass?"

"We have several ma'am, I'll bring you a wine list."

"Thank you Ashley."

Ashley returned to the table with both the wine list and Lynie. Lynie had grown into such a beautiful young lady. She was studying English at Spelman, following in my footsteps, and I couldn't be more proud.

"Sissy," Lynie shouted with a huge smile and open arms.

I jumped up to hug her and gave her a kiss on the cheek. "You got here quickly. Were you on campus?"

"Actually I was right around the corner at Lenox Square. We have convocation tomorrow and I needed a new pair of flesh tone stockings."

We both giggled. Neither of us liked the idea of wearing flesh tone stockings. The fact that she had to do the same

thing that my girls and I had to do years ago made me reminisce about my time at Spelman. I had to get new flesh tone
stockings almost every week for Convocation because I could
never seem to get a pair of stockings to last more than a day.

Each Wednesday for convocation we had to put on white
dresses, flesh tone stockings, and black shoes. It was the
worst. Lynie settled into the seat that was across from me so
she could check out the view as well. "I was about to order a
glass of champagne but, since you're here are you going to be
drinking champagne as well because if so we can get a bottle
of instead."

"That would be great. I'm in the middle of exams and I
can't wait until all of this is over."

"In due time my dear. It will be over in due time. So, what
have you been up to?"

"Not a whole lot to be honest. It's really been just studying and trying to get a handle on all of these classes that I
have."

"Humph, you have been doing a little more than studying," I said with a smirk. Lynie looked at me with her eyebrows
raised.

"I got a visitor at my school yesterday."

Lynie's bright eyes widened with anticipation. "He didn't,"
she gasped.

"Yes, honey, he did."

"Oh my God, tell me all about it."

"Well apparently, after you shared with him where Mama
and Daddy's car lot was, he went by and had a conversation
with them." Lynie listened to me intently as I recounted
the story of him showing up at the car lot the same day
that I had been in court with Christian for the restraining

order and the assault charges. I also told her about him showing up at the school. "Those biddies that work with me were gawking at him as he stood in the lobby waiting on me to come and get him. I was so embarrassed Lynie. I know they're going to have a ton of questions for me when I get to work on Monday."

"Oh screw them Kami."

"Easy for you to say honey, you're at a different point in your life than I am. I am a married woman. Christian, remember, your brother-in-law…."

"Well in my opinion Kami, it's about time that he gets a little taste of his own medicine. You have been so good to him and all he has done is disrespect you. I don't see a problem with an old friend looking you up. You could use someone to cheer you up given all you've been through."

"Given all that I've been through, I actually feel pretty good today. I'm not sure if it was the spa treatments I had just a few minutes ago or the fact that I'm having lunch with you but, whatever it is my spirits are like on 10."

"No, you're just excited about the fact that you just saw William again." Playfully I smacked Lynie and we giggled like little schoolgirls. When Ashley returned we decided to order a few appetizers for the table and lunch. I had my mouth set on the salmon that was stuffed with spinach and crab meat. Lynie decided to get the quesadillas and a salad. After polishing off our first bottle of champagne Lynie and I were feeling really good. "William left you his number. Are you going to call him?

"I don't think that's a good idea Lynie. What am I going to say?"

"Say Hi." Lynie said with a giggle. "No seriously honey, I'm going to say this- you and William have always been really good friends Kami. I'm more than sure that the two of you can figure out what to say to each other. As a matter of fact, I think you need to call him now. This is the perfect time for you all to see each other. I mean- I'm here. If anybody were to see us sitting here they wouldn't know who he was with."

I thought for a minute about Lynie's proposition and the prospect of William sitting at the table with my sister and I on the patio at Brio where everyone in Atlanta could see. It's mighty funny that before I left the house I had taken his number out of my workbag and put it in my purse. I think deep down I knew that I was going to eventually call him. So, after another few moments, constant ribbing from Lynie and several glasses of champagne, I had what I would like to call *liquid courage*. I picked up my cell phone and dialed the number. Before I had a chance to reconsider, William picked up the phone.

"Hello," he said.

"Hey, you."

"If someone is saying 'hey you' on my phone it can only be one person. How's it going Kami?"

"Wonderful. Lynie and I are sitting on the patio at Brio on Peachtree Street. Would you like to join us?"

"The stars must be aligned," William said. "I happen to be right up the street. I just finished having a meeting with my attorney and so I'm literally only about 5 minutes away. I would love to join the two of you. See you in a minute."

William hung up the phone and then I gently place my phone back on the table and looked up at Lynie. "Look at the mess that you're getting me into," I said with a smile on my face.

"I'm not getting you into anything. Again, I see nothing wrong with old friends sitting down and having cocktails." "Lynie, you and I both know that William and I were way more than friends."

"That may be true but, I think you need a little diversion right now Kami."

Just as Lynie and I were about to get into it, I caught a glimpse of a man entering the patio area out the corner of my eye. I could tell by the way women were stopping to stare that it must be William. He had that effect on people. Whenever he entered the room, all eyes would be on him. I can remember when we were in college and we would go out together it was almost as if we were parting the Red Sea as we walked into any room, any restaurant, or the mall for that matter. People would gawk at us.

Lynie jumped out of her chair and squealed as she ran over to give him a hug and brought him to the table. I was more reserved because I was still getting over the fact that I had actually called and invited him to have lunch with us. They made their way around the fountain and over to the table. I got up and gave William a hug after which he settled into his seat at the table. For the first few minutes, Lynie and William laughed and recapped their conversation at the mall. Lynie said, "I knew you were up to something when you asked where Mama and Daddy were and how they were doing. You know Daddy has a big mouth and you knew that as soon as you got him talking he was going to give you all the information that you wanted and needed."

"I have to admit, I did know that Dad was going to give up the info," William said with a giggle.

"Go ahead. Laugh it up," I said. "You two are not the ones that are going to have to deal with a bunch of chatty colleagues on Monday morning when you get to school. We all laughed and continued to drink, snack, and reminisce about old times.

Before any of us realized it was already 6 o'clock. We had spent the entire afternoon relaxing in the sunshine enjoying each other's company. I didn't want it to end. Lynie looked down at her watch and said, "It's about that time for me to head back to the dorm. My roommate and I are planning to spend some time with a few guys that we met the other afternoon on campus. So, I hate to eat and run but, it's time for me to break this camp and let you two old folks spend some time together. "

"Old folks," I said as I cut my eyes at her. "I think it's time for me to go as well. It's getting late. William, thank you so much for coming out. I really enjoyed our time together."

I wasn't expecting it but, William paid the bill, we thanked him and we all got up and headed to the valet for our cars. My car came first. I hugged William, kissed Lynie on the cheek, and I hopped in my car. I made a right out of the parking lot of Brio and headed toward downtown. Sometimes, I enjoy taking the streets instead of the highway so I can take in the city skyline. It was such a beautiful evening and I yearned for just a little bit more of the setting sun and the clean crisp air before I headed home.

As I approached the first stoplight, I heard my cell phone buzzing. I looked down at the screen. It was a text message from William. It read, "It was so good to see you. I'm not ready for the night to end and I want to spend some time with you alone."

I pulled my car over in the Publix parking lot and I sat there for a few seconds, contemplating whether I was going to respond. I knew that if I said yes that I was opening a huge can of worms.

I was opening Pandora's Box.

Once that box was opened, I knew it would be very difficult to close it. After a slight pause, I text back, "What do you have in mind?"

Christian was out of town and Ethan was with his Nana. What else did I have to do? I would just be sitting at home twiddling my thumbs. Why not have a little fun with a sexy friend. It was happy hour and he offered to drive. So I decided to park my car in the Publix parking lot, put my top up, and wait for William to arrive. I saw the lights of his black Benz turn into the parking lot and navigate over to where I was parked. He rolled down his window and I in turn rolled down mine.

"Waiting on someone beautiful?" he asked with a sexy smile.

I stared at William contemplating whether I was going to get into his car or, if it was better a better idea for me to just drive off now and forget that I had ever agreed. He unlocked his door. I decided that since I had made it this far, I needed to just put my big girl panties on and go with the flow. I rolled up the window to my car, hopped out, locked my car door, and slid into the passenger seat of William's car.

As we pulled off, he retracted the sunroof a little further and headed back into Buckhead so we could take in the sights and the sounds of the city while listening to Sade's *No Ordinary Love*. We decided to have drinks and dinner at Sambuca, a Jazz Supper Club of sorts that played live music nightly. It was an elegant but relaxed atmosphere where professionals from all over the city came to network and eat while listening to some good music. "Oh wow, Meshell Ndegeocello is performing. She is one of my favorite artists. I can't believe I wasn't aware she was in Atlanta."

William smiled, "Stick with me, I'll show you lots." My face flushed.

As we entered Sambuca the young lady at the hostess stand in the reception area smiled at William and nodded at us to follow. I was trying to figure out how we were already being seated when there were droves of people waiting in the lobby for tables. Apparently William had made friends with some of the individuals that were here and so he was on their "priority" list.

We settled into an amazing booth with full view of the stage. We sipped wine and were enraptured by the sweet sound of music that floated through the air. William and I spent the evening catching up, laughing and talking about our lives to this point. I shared with him many of the gruesome details of my last few months with Christian. He shared with me that after I decided to get married that he went back to Michelle and decided to do the same saying, "At least I knew she had my back. She was there before the contracts, glitz and glamour."

It was interesting how both of us had made choices in our lives that directly impacted whether or not we would be able to be together. He was married to Michelle and I was married to Christian, and yet there was still this pull between us. William put his arm around the back of the booth. His hand gently grazed my shoulder. This made me a bit uncomfortable and so, I turned to William and said, "Look William, I'm really weak right now and I cannot afford to make the situation between Christian and I any worse than it is already."

"If nothing else Kami, I can be your friend," William said. "I can never repay you and your family for what you all did for me while I was in school. The least I can do is be here for you right now. I know things are rough and I know that you need a friend."

I smiled at William and said, "I'll think about it." I glanced down at my watch and realized it was already after midnight. The band had long since stopped playing. Where had the time gone? I looked at William and before I could say anything he said, "I know, it's time for you to go right?"

"Yes William. I think it's time for me to go."

William paid the check and we headed out to the car. Our ride back to the Publix parking lot was relatively silent but peaceful at the same time. I think we were both processing the evening. I glanced over at William, took in his side profile and then looked forward. I could see out of the corner of my eye that he was looking at me. He had this way of looking at you that made you feel like he was looking through you and could actually see your soul. I tried to pretend that I didn't notice and continued to look forward.

As we got closer to Publix I felt myself relaxing. We pulled into the Publix parking lot and I was happy to see that my car was still there. Things in Atlanta had gotten pretty weird with all of the stuff that was happening in the Buckhead area. William pulled his car next to mine and placed it in park. "Kami I'm serious about what I said at Sambuca. I'm here for you if you need me and I want to see you again."

I smiled, acknowledging William's offer, but I didn't respond as to whether or not anything would happen. "I can see I'm not going to get an answer from you this evening but, since you called me, I now have your phone number. I hope you don't mind if I check on you from time to time?"

"That would be fine," I said. "It is always good to hear from you William." William smiled and unlocked the door so that I could get out of the car. "Text me when you get to the house. I want to know you made it safely. We've done a lot of drinking this evening and so I'm going to be worried if I don't hear from you." I kissed him on the cheek and jumped out of the car before he had an opportunity to reciprocate. I glanced back at him over my shoulder with a stunning yet mischievous smile hopped into my car and drove home.

DECEMBER 23, 1992

"**K**ami darling," Mama yelled from the kitchen.
"Yes Ma'am."
"Come hold this pan for me while I transfer the cornbread dressing from this pot."

"K." I collected myself from my spot on the sofa next to William. The winter holiday season was always exciting in our household. The festivities began in November with a huge family dinner at Auntie Mina's and continued on through the New Year. Hell, every weekend was an opportunity to get together with family and friends to eat and fellowship. The holidays just gave us a reason.

Mama would start prepping for our Christmas feast about two weeks before Christmas. It was her favorite time of year and our house showed it. It was decorated from the "roota to the tootta" as Grandma would say, with every room having its own theme. Lights twinkling softly above the crackling fireplace added a warm glow to the room.

The dorms at both Spelman and Georgia Tech were closed for winter break. William's family, his mom rather, didn't have the money to send for him for Christmas this year so the decision had been made that he would stay at our house for winter break.

William watched everyone scurrying around preparing for what was sure to be a fabulous feast. "What can I do to help?"

"The best thing for us to do is to try to stay out of the way and be ready to jump into action when Mama or Daddy calls us."

"I see," William said as he took in the scene. "I just feel funny not helping. I want your parents to know how much I appreciate them having me here. I don't take this for granted at all."

"We know you don't. That's part of the reason they allowed you to stay. But, you know Mama, she likes things done a certain way," I said with a giggle and a smirk. William agreed joining me in laughter. "She always goes out of her way to please everyone," I continued.

"Everyone?" he teased. I ticked off on my fingers

"This year the menu includes everything from Crawfish ettoufee to cornbread dressing, turkey, roast, ham, and potato salad. Do you know how to make any of that?" I asked sarcastically. William gave me a blank stare trying to intimidate and hold in his laughter until neither of us could hold it in any longer and both began to cackle loudly.

As we giggled and settled into a movie in the family room, my sisters snooped around the house trying the figure out where their presents were hidden so that they could confirm whether they had gotten anything off of their Christmas list.

Mama and Daddy continued in the kitchen working together as they always did trying to put the finishing touches on some of the food items on our list before they had to stop in order to get ready for a dinner party at the Duncan's house that evening.

William and I had been told that we would be watching over my sisters, however, they ended up being invited to a sleepover at their friend Chloe's house. Since they were only fifteen months apart, where one went the other always followed closely behind. So, that evening ended up being a time where William and I were alone for the first time at my parent's home.

"You know, my parents have never allowed a male to stay over here."

"That's a good thing," William asserted. "Besides, who could deny me? Everyone loves me."

I playfully punched him in the arm and he pretended to take cover.

William had become quite close to our family over the past few months.

His open and infectious personality had broken down any barriers my parents could put up. He was the kind of person that made you love him and want to be around him. Mama and Daddy felt compassion for his situation, and were comfortable having him around.

As everyone else prepared for their evening away from home, William and I prepared for our evening at home. We could easily have gone out to the movies or gone to hang with friends that were also home for the holidays, but instead we decided we would stay home and help my parents wrap my sisters' Christmas presents. With them out of the house, it was the perfect opportunity.

Once we were alone, William began to pull the gifts from the attic, the one place my sisters hadn't looked, and stacked them in the family room. He then brought in all of the wrapping paper and supplies that we needed in order to get the job done.

While he worked, I made a pot of hot chocolate, hoping to add a bit of sweetness to the arduous task we had before us. I picked up the two marshmallow capped mugs and joined William in the family room. Just the mere sight of the gifts and wrapping paper made me smile.

"I love wrapping presents."

"I can tell by that huge grin you have on your face. What's all of this?" William asked.

"In order to make each gift special and unique, I pick up trinkets over the course of the year to add to the tops of each present I wrap. It's one of the only times that I really get to allow my creative side to shine through."

William listened intently learning a little more about me and how I had been raised with each word.

"The wrapping is always far more exquisite than the gift inside," I said with a tiny chuckle.

"In our household, our parents raised us with the understanding that Christmas is Jesus's birthday, a time to give. Big gifts are reserved for our birthdays."

"I love how your family is Kami. You guys really enjoy each other. Even if you all only have a little there is a lot of love in this house. My Mama did the best she could with what she had" his voice trailing off a bit. My brother and I know she loves us. She works so hard and tries to put us in the best situations possible. Even with that, things have been hard. Thank goodness I was accepted into private school. That kept me out of trouble and positioned me for the football scholarship I now have at Georgia Tech. My dream is to be able to take care of her one day. I don't want her to have to struggle any more."

William and I continued with our task talking and listening to music until we got all of the presents wrapped and under the tree. It took way longer than we expected. In fact, it was almost eleven o'clock p.m. when we finally finished everything we had been asked to do. After all of that, relaxation was definitely in order.

We settled in on the sofa to finish watching the movie we had started earlier in the day. Although we had seen *Boys in the Hood* many times before it always helped us to keep things in perspective.

"I swear to God that I can relate to every single thing that these kids go through in the movie," William said.

I wasn't sure whether he was stretching the truth or not but I did know that he hadn't come from the best of neighborhoods.

"Hmmmm," I said as William wrapped his arms around me. I snuggled under his armpit. A few months earlier, I would have never allowed him to hold me like this. Cuddling... Are you kidding me? That was completely out of the question then, but William had shown me something different. Despite my efforts to push him away he continued to remain present and show me how much he cared about me. He didn't allow anyone to come in between us and if he felt like they were going to be an issue he dealt with them immediately, male or female. I was beginning to trust him. His consistency was allowing him to break through the cocoon that had been wrapped around my heart.

I could smell him. He always smelled fresh and clean except of course when he came off that football field. Hugs would be far and few between then.

William gently caressed the back of my neck and planted a gentle wet kiss on my forehead.

"Kami, I just want to thank you again for taking me in. I know your Mom and Dad don't necessarily approve of you having young men stay over. I really appreciate them and you for doing this for me.

"William, I don't want you to think another second about that, darling. As you know by now, our home is your home."

"It was bad enough thinking that I was going to have to spend Christmas at the dorm. I've never been apart from my family at Christmas. Despite the fact that it has been very difficult for Mom, she always figured out a way to get me a ticket for the holidays. With my little brother coming up very close behind me, I knew that it was going to be hard for her to swing it this year."

"Mama and Daddy love you. They want you here as much as I do."

William planted another kiss on my forehead and I turned my head upward to look at him. He was beautiful. I could see the joy and pain in his eyes. I tilted my head upward to give him a kiss.

As my lips touched his, I could feel his tongue tickling the tiny opening that had formed between my lips.

My tongue met his and danced a slow sensual jig. It was on.

All bets of being good were off, and there were no holds barred.

We were completely free.

William unbuttoned the top button of my blouse and kissed my neck. I leaned my head back.

"Relax," he said, unbuttoning his way down to my waist.

"You too," I said with a smile. I pulled his t-shirt up over his head.

His caramel skin was silk and his muscles bulged in all the right places. His neck, although athletic, was graceful and refined like his jaw line. I gently kissed the lobe of his ear and deeply inhaled his scent. "You smell so good," I said.

I could feel William's body responding to my touch. We were enraptured in the moment. Enraptured in us.

"Come here," he said, and pulled me onto his lap.

I straddled him. His manhood expanded against me, growing bigger and bigger, longer and longer.

"Is that for me," I asked with a mischievous grin.

"Yea, that is all for you," he responded

We sat on the floor in front of the fireplace, kissing each other as if we had just realized that this was where each of us should be.

He began to kiss and caress my back, my hands, and my breasts. In one smooth sensual motion, he laid me on my back and slid my panties to the side to access my special spot. His tongue teasingly danced on top of my clitoris activating a volcano of passion and anticipation inside of me. His tongue continued to tease and please me taking me to places I never knew I could go. My body trembled as I gasped for air and grabbed at the floor trying to regain control and composure. There was no hope. William was relentless and would not bow down until he got what he wanted. With one final lick and suckle, my body erupted releasing my lava into his mouth.

In one swift motion, lips still attached to my special place, William lifted me up in the air and lowered me on top of his manhood. I could feel every inch of him as I rocked back and forth, slowly teasing the tip and then consuming the mass while circling my hips around and around. No one could have pried us apart. I rode him as if it was our last race.

We reached ecstasy together that night on the floor as our bodies erupted over and over again in front of the fireplace.

It was so perfect. We were perfect.

OCTOBER 4, 1997

The dashboard clock of the BMW displayed 6:30 p.m. when I pulled up to Kirby's house to scoop her up for the concert. Since freshman year at Spelman, we had been best friends and hanging partners. Kirby was still enjoying the single life flitting happily from flower to flower and, despite my marriage to Christian, I still managed to carve out time to spend with her and the girls. Marriage and motherhood had not stopped me one bit, especially with all of Christian transgressions.

The Mary J. Blige concert at Chastain Park was scheduled to begin promptly at seven thirty. With weekend traffic in Atlanta, and Kirby's tortoise like pace, we were definitely going to be late. Thank goodness there were a few opening acts. Lord knows it would be a good eight thirty before we got to the park, parked the car and made it to our seats.

I swear *she's going to be late for her own funeral.*

It had become the norm for us to arrive when the festivities were wrapping up, no matter where we were going. Never mind the fact that we had paid almost three hundred dollars per ticket for pit seats, I was sure it would be the same ole story.

"Ugh," I mumbled, hopping out of the car. Kirby must have seen me coming up the path because before I could ring the bell she opened the front door still rocking her robe and slippers with a piece of tissue hanging out of her right nostril. She had the worst allergies ever. Year round, she was always sniffling and grunting.

"Hey girl. I am almost ready. I just have to throw on my dress, change purses and throw on my shoes"

"What have you been doing Kirby? That was what you were supposed to be doing two hours ago."

"Well see, what happened was Mama called and I was talking to her and getting ready at the same time."

"You and I both know you can't talk and get dressed at the same time. We are always late for everything." I said in a huff as I settled down on the sofa in the front room of Kirby's house. Her home was small and eclectic. Furnished with many of her father's original paintings donning the walls. Bursts of orange, blue and yellow filled each room adding to the ethereal beauty of the quaint space. "It's already seven, Kirby" I yelled.

"Coming," Kirby responded as she bounded into the front room hopping on one leg until she placed her right shoe on her naked foot.

"Can we please do something about that tissue in your nose?"

"Girl, my allergies have just been so bad. I promise I will take it out," she said as she transferred items from her tote to a smaller more manageable handbag.

"Is there anything I can help you do so we can get out of here?"

"I'm ready" she said as she grabbed her keys off of the dining room table, set the alarm, and headed to the door.

I was right on her heels seeing as though the show had started fifteen minutes ago.

At eight thirty on the nose, we shuffled to our seats just as Mary walked onstage. Mary J Blige had been to our city tons of times but no matter how often, I never missed a show and she never failed to bring it. Kirby and I jumped up, singing and dancing throughout her entire set. She ended the show with her song "Real Love."

As we sang along Kirby asked with a giggle, "Speaking of *Real Love*, have you heard from William?"

"I have," I responded with a coy smile as if not to divulge any further information.

"Oh you have huh? When were you planning to tell me?" Kirby asked pretending to have an attitude.

I giggled and responded, "Lynie and I hung out with him at Brio the other week and we have been talking and texting a lot ever since."

"I haven't seen him in years," Kirby said. "Since it's still early, we should hit him and see what he is getting into tonight."

"See. You and Lynie. Y'all two are always getting me into some shit."

"Stop acting like you don't want to reach out to him," Kirby snapped back.

With Kirby looking over my shoulder, I texted,

"Hey you. Feel like hanging out?"

Before I could put my phone back in my purse, William immediately texted back, "Hey Baby. My boy Jesse and I are at the Shark Bar. Where are you?"

Kirby and I giggled like two schoolgirls as I replied, "We are about to leave the Mary J concert. Not sure where we are headed."

Quickly William responded, "You two should meet us here."

I showed Kirby the screen and with a big smile on my face I asked, "You down?"

"Let's roll," Kirby replied.

I messaged William, "Kirby and I are on our way," as we collected our belongings and headed toward the car.

There was bumper-to-bumper traffic on Peachtree Street around the Shark Bar. Since we were arriving later than usual, it was going to be a bitch finding parking. Everyone was out and about. Cars were honking as groups of guys and girls ran across the street in front of them.

"Girl, we probably aren't going to be able to get in there," Kirby said observing the spectacle.

"I agree. Reach in my purse and grab my phone. Call William and let him know this is too much and we are not going to be able to get to him."

Kirby grabbed my phone out of my bag and dialed William's number on speaker.

"Hey Baby," William answered on the first ring.

"This isn't baby," Kirby responded with a laugh.

"Oh, Hey Kirby, I thought you were Kami."

"She's driving but can hear you," Kirby responded.

"Hey William, I don't think we are going to be able to find parking or get into the Shark Bar. The streets are slammed and there is a line wrapped around the building to get in there."

"All you have to do is drive up front. I gave the valet your name. He will take care of your car. Then just walk up to the front of the line, my boy Block is waiting on you two."

Kirby and I exchanged looks trying to decide if we wanted to go in or not. With so much activity going on in the city there were plenty after-hour options to choose from. Since this was such a popular spot, I wasn't sure if William and I should be caught there together.

"William, with our situations, I think this is a bit much. I'm not sure we want to be on blast quite like this."

"I see your point, there is another option, but I am not sure if you would feel comfortable with that either."

"What is it William, whatever we are going to do, we need to decided quickly, I am tired of circling the block."

"Michelle and the boys are out of the country for the next two weeks, you and Kirby are welcome to come over."

"I don't know about that, William."

"It will be you, Kirby, Jesse, a few other people and I. No funny stuff, I promise."

Kirby and I looked at each other again. "What do you think," I mouthed so William couldn't hear.

"We should be good. It's a group, Kirby mouthed in response.

"Ok, let's do that" I responded.

"Ok, let me close out my tab and we will be right out. You can follow me to my house. I am in my Benz. You remember what it looks like?" He said. I could hear his smile through the phone.

"Yes William, I remember," I responded sarcastically.

"Pull up to the valet and wait for me there. Let them know who you are and that I am coming out."

I pulled my car up to the valet and rolled down the window.

"Good Evening Ma'am will you be parking with us this is evening?"

"No sir, I am Kameleon Beck a guest of William Levy's. He is on his way out."

"Oh yes Ma'am, his Benz is parked right there, just pull right behind him. You will be fine there."

Kirby and I exchanged glances and smiles once more as we did what we were told. Within minutes, William exited the Shark Bar heading straight for us with a crew following him.

"Hey Baby, hey Miss Kirby, long time no see."

"Hello kind sir," Kirby responded with a smile. "I see you run this place."

"No, I just spend a lot of money here that's all. That comes with a few privileges," he said with his dashing smile. "Baby, are you sure you're ok with the plan? I just want to make sure you're all right and I want you to be completely comfortable."

"I am fine William. As long as there is a group and you promise to be on your best behavior, I feel comfortable."

"I promise."

"Ok, cool, then let's go."

While Jesse, Kirby and the crew were talking shit to each other about who was going to beat who in cards, William and I slipped into the billiards room.

Despite the millions he had made over the years playing ball, his home was modest, and I loved it.

The walls were flanked with all of his jerseys from each of the teams he had played for, as well as every award he had received throughout his career. Laid out on the pool table were some drawings.

"Come here, I wanna show you something," William said. He pointed to the drawings. "This is a part of my retirement plan," he said with a chuckle. "These are the renderings of a shopping mall I am constructing. I decided to take some of my money and invest it in commercial real estate."

His face lit up as he discussed the project and described all of the potential businesses that were interested in the project. William was always good with a dollar, and I knew that he wouldn't be like many pro players who squander away their earnings within the first year and end up broke when it was all said and done.

We talked until I could see daylight peeking through the windows of the billiards room.

"Oh my God, William, it's daylight." I grabbed for my cell phone, but it was dead.

"I have to go." I ran to the other room to get Kirby who had dozed off on the sofa with her cards in her hands. Everyone else was splattered across the floor and the sofas asleep as well.

"Kirby. Wake up. It's daylight." I shook her until she finally began to stir. Sleepily, Kirby pulled herself from the sofa and grabbed her handbag. William helped to see us out.

"Thank you for coming by Kami. I really enjoyed catching up with you. Are you sure you're going to be ok? I mean, time got away from us and I hadn't planned on keeping you out this late. I hope this doesn't cause you too much trouble," William said with a worried expression on his face.

"Christian will have questions I am sure, but I will be fine. Thanks for the invite. I really enjoyed catching up with you as well. Sorry I have to speed off like this," I said. "I will reach out to you when the dust settles," I yelled through the window as Kirby and I climbed in the car. William smiled then waved and retreated into his home watching us as we pulled off through the windows of the front door.

I plugged my phone into the car charger and as it powered up, I saw twenty messages from Christian. Although I considered ignoring him and doing one of his numbers by just showing up at the house like it was no big deal. I knew better. I had to call him and tell him something. I'd have to lie.

"Kameleon, where are you?" Christian asked.

"I was too tipsy to drive home and I passed out at Kirby's house."

I don't think Christian believed me. He simply responded, "Oh, ok."

There was something in his tone that tipped me off and let me know we had to boogie. Kirby and I flew like hell back to her house. As we approached her street, I saw Christian's black BMW 6 series rounding the corner on two wheels.

"Oh shit Kami. That's Christian," Kirby yelled finally awake from her slumber. "What are we going to do?"

I sped past the street and headed for I-20 back toward my house. Kirby called Dia, who had been babysitting Ethan, and told her to grab two t-shirts and put them out for us. Everyone who knows me knows that I drive like a turtle but not today. I had never driven so fast before in my life. I had the pedal of my car to the floor and I was not letting up. We made it to my house in Stone Mountain from downtown Atlanta in ten minutes.

Dia met us at the door and just said, "Oh shit."

She knew we had been up to something. She grinned as she described how mad Christian had been when he left the house. "He was pacing back and forth in the front room grumbling something under his breath. He even stood over my shoulder to see if you called me. When I tried to call you, it went to voicemail."

"Yea, my phone was dead."

Seconds later we heard the garage door open.

Christian burst through the back door with fire in his eyes.

When he saw that we were all sitting in there with our t-shirts and sweats he calmed down.

Even if it was a farce, I think he was relieved that at least I was home.

"Umm hmmm, that car of yours is mighty hot out there" Christian said.

"Yea honey I jumped in it and flew home once I talked to you. I was too tipsy to drive all the way home last night so I passed out at Kirby's."

Christian looked over at Kirby who was nodding and giggling in agreement. "Yea, Christian, we were like 'oh shit'."

He said, "Oh shit is right. I better not find out that anything else was going on last night."

"I'm not you, Christian."

Everyone looked away.

A little remorse crept in because I knew I was lying, but in my mind he deserved a little of his own medicine.

The phone rang and Christian said, "Hey B, what's up? What," Christian gasped.

"Christian what's wrong," I asked as I watched tears forming in his eyes.

He tried to collect himself and tell me but nothing would come out.

"I grabbed the phone from Christian and asked, "B what's wrong? What's going on?"

"Oh my God."

Dia and Kirby looked on, frightened to ask what was happening.

"I dropped the phone and said, "Christian's Dad was just rushed to the hospital. Braxton and Heidi found him on his bathroom floor. He is having difficulty breathing. The doctors are saying he doesn't look good. Christian we need to get to the hospital now."

Christian's father, Louis, was my rock. We spent a lot of time together. Before Christian and I married, he lived with his father, so his dad got a chance to watch our relationship grow. He nurtured us throughout our courtship and had comforted me through our recent struggles.

Louis had been sick for some time, but over the past few months, his health had been deteriorating more rapidly.

Since my schedule was the most flexible, I had been taking him to all of his doctor appointments. Louis and I were really close.

"Oh, Christian. Just last week he had been given a good prognosis. I thought things were turning around." Tears welled up in my eyes.

"I thought so too, Kami."

Christian and I went into overdrive, throwing on clothes and pulling together a few things to head to the hospital.

"Dia please take Kirby home. Girl, I don't want you stranded over here through this."

"I really don't mind Kami. Dia and I can watch Ethan and make sure he's good for the evening."

"I'll let you two decide how you want to handle that," I said, hugging them both. "Christian and I have to go."

"Keep us posted," they yelled as we raced out the door toward the hospital.

Heidi, Braxton's wife met us at the doors of the emergency room and took us back to Louis's room.

"How's he doing," Christian asked

"Christian, he doesn't look like himself."

Heidi dropped her eyes, then looked at me. "He's extremely swollen and is hooked up to everything known to man. I don't want you two to be shocked when you walk in. He just asked for you Christian."

We entered the room and saw Louis lying in the center of the room in the hospital bed. He was so swollen we could see the fluid erupting up against his skin. His eyes were closed. Machines surrounded the bed. One of them was helping him breathe.

We stood next to the bed in silence for a minute, watching his chest rise and fall in an automated fashion and listening to the faint sound of the respirator.

Louis's eyes fluttered. He gasped for air as he reached for Christian and said in a soft voice that broke my heart, "You made it."

"Yes Dad, Kami and I are both here," Christian said.

Louis coughed as he tried to gain his breath. He clutched Christian's hand. In a raspy whisper, he said, "Christian, I love you. You see that lady standing next to you?"

"Yes." Christian said.

"I love her too. If you don't do anything else in your life son, you take care of her and your child."

Louis's stare was piercing and his eyes were sharp and focused on Christian. Then he looked at me.

I had the feeling that he could see through us and all that we had going on inside our marriage. I dropped my head, thinking about my transgressions from the night before. *Who was I becoming?*

"I will Dad, I promise I will," Christian said, his voice cracking. "We're going to get through this, Dad. Don't give up," Christian said.

"Christian, I'm tired, and I'm ready," Louis said. "Look at me. I have no quality of life." His hand trembled and he withdrew it from Christian's and fumbled with the sheet covering his body. "I've been walking around with that damn oxygen tank for the last five years and I'm sick of it."

"I don't understand. The doctor said you were improving," Christian said.

"Ah hog wash," Louis said, more like his old self. "He told me last month that it wouldn't be long. I asked him not to share it with you and Braxton."

A tear rolled down Christian's face as he stood over his father, his face grimacing with pain.

Louis once stood at six two and weighed two hundred pounds, but right now he looked so frail and weak lying in that hospital bed that I wanted to look away.

Braxton and Heidi joined Christian and I at Louis's bedside.

"Dad, would you like for us to pray with you," I asked.

Louis nodded yes.

The five of us bowed our heads and began to pray the Hail Mary.

Hail Mary.

Full of Grace, The Lord is with Thee

Blessed art thou among women

And blessed is the fruit of thy womb, Jesus

Holy Mary, Mother of God

Pray for us sinners,

Now and at the hour of our death

Amen

Surrounded by his small family, and holding his son's hands, Louis Joseph Beck took his final breath.

FEBRUARY 12, 1993

"**B**abe, what's wrong? Why are you so quiet? You seem preoccupied," William said.

I sat in the passenger seat trying to decide what to tell him and how. "I'm late."

"What do you mean you're late?"

"My cycle didn't come last month and it hasn't come yet for this month."

William stared at the road ahead of him. When he brought his Jeep to a stop at a traffic light, I wasn't sure whether he was concerned about something in the road or whether he was trying to compose himself. It scared me.

"You think you're pregnant," he said.

"I'm never late. If my period isn't here on time, it means only one thing," I said.

We sat in silence at the light for a few minutes. It must have been longer than I thought because the car behind us got frustrated and honked.

Startled by the other driver's impatience, William took off causing us both to jerk forward. "Sorry about that Kami,

What do you want to do?" William asked glancing at me before turning his attention back to the road.

"I'm really not sure William. I already told you how I feel about abortion. I went through that all alone in high school, and I said I would never do that again. Now here I am in the same situation all over again except this time, I knew what we were doing." I looked out the window at the students walking toward campus from the Marta station on Lee Street. They all looked so happy and carefree.

"I knew if we had unprotected sex we might get pregnant. How could I be so careless," I said, moaning.

"Kami, I knew what we were doing too," William said. "I love you and if it's meant for us to have a child now, then so be it."

"We both have so much at stake William," I said. "You're about to be drafted to the NFL in a few months and you don't need this hanging over your head as you start your career. I've been interning with the local television station and I'm planning to enter grad school after graduation. Neither of us can afford this to happen right now." A tear fell from my eye. I was completely overwhelmed.

The severity of the situation and the decision before us hit me as we sat talking. Two years ago, I was so hardened that nothing really mattered to me. I would have made the decision without even consulting William. However, over the last two years, William and I had been through so much together and shared so much that I couldn't dream of making a decision this important without him. Feelings were involved and I needed him to be with me whatever the decision.

William's car approached the back gate of Spelman, and I gathered my things. I opened the passenger door, and

William said, "Kami you know I'm here for you. You're not in this alone. If you need anything or just want to talk call me, we can talk on the phone or I'll come get you."

"I'll call you later," I told him, wearied with emotion. I kissed him on the cheek and jumped out of the jeep.

As I walked through the huge iron back gate toward my dorm, I imagined what my life would be like if I had a child right now. I thought about my mother and how all of her dreams were deferred when she decided to have me. I really wanted to talk to her about it, but I knew I couldn't.

My parents had already been through this with me one time before and I didn't want them to be any further disappointed in me. Tears streamed down my face as I surrendered to my thoughts; thoughts of my future, thoughts of William's future, thoughts of my parents and thoughts of our unborn child.

FEBRUARY 19, 1993

The dingy green walls of the clinic closed in on me, and a strong smell of stale ammonia bit my nose as we walked in. Doctor's offices have a distinct smell you could pick out even if you're blindfolded.

The chairs lined up against the wall of the lobby were filled with lost and disenfranchised looking women. They faced the reception window and the chubby, cherub-faced lady behind the glass working on her computer. On the far side of the room were a set of double stainless-steel doors.

The atmosphere was somber. I tugged at William's shirt. "This isn't the place for us," I whispered.

Our futures were bright. We were always so happy. But, I had to admit, today we were heavy with emotion. Thoughts of what we were going to do consumed me. It leveled the playing field and grounded us. We were no different from anyone else in that room that afternoon. We quickly signed in and sat down at the end of the row of chairs.

This is a place where women reclaim their lives and get another chance at their dreams, I thought.

However we'd arrived here, this was the opportunity to do better. But, was it really an opportunity? Or, was it adding to the emotional baggage we all carried.

When you enter this kind of place you think you're changing things. By pressing reset, you think you're regaining your control. You think you can put it all behind you and that perhaps there is a chance that you may be able to achieve some of the dreams and goals that you set for yourself.

"Kameleon Papillon," the cherub-faced lady called.

"I placed my tote on William's lap and got up.

"You want me to come up with you babe," William asked.

"No, I'm fine."

At the glass window, the lady, whose nametag identified her as Elaine handed me a stack of papers on a clipboard. "Complete both the front and back of each page, hon" she said.

I took the clipboard and pen and returned to my seat next to William.

His normally relaxed faced was riddled with frown lines and the little vein that popped out of the side of his neck whenever he was nervous was pulsating. He rubbed his hands together and clenched them like he did when he was applying lotion. He was clearly as uncomfortable as I was.

I admired his courage. He refused to allow me to go through this alone and he promised that he was going to be with me every step of the way regardless of our decision. Over the past week, we had spent a lot of time talking about the possibility of keeping our child, but, deep down we knew we were not ready to be parents. We couldn't even take care of ourselves. How were we going to take care of a newborn?

"This is the best decision for both of us at this time," we told each other.

Neither of us had the courage that our mothers did when they were our age.

I completed the intake papers, answering as many questions as I could; and then quickly slid the papers behind the glass before I could change my mind.

As I turned to walk away, the cherub-faced lady said, "Dear you don't have to return to your seat. We're ready for you now."

I glanced at William and then back at her.

She smiled and asked, "Do you have anyone here with you?"

"Yes ma'am, I do," I said.

"Would you like them to come back with you?"

I motioned for William to gather our things and join me at the desk.

The cherub-faced lady pressed a buzzer, unlocking the door that led to the patient rooms.

We walked through the large steel door and were greeted on the inside by a nurse who introduced herself and led us towards the back of the clinic to a small room.

Before she left, she asked me to take my clothes off and put on the open gown that she had placed on the table.

William helped me pull off my clothes and slip into the robe. It was huge, and swallowed my tiny frame. He then gently hoisted me up on the table and covered me with the blanket.

This was not a happy place. I could feel the spirits of those who had come before me whispering to me. Telling me their whys.

I laid down on the exam table and tried to drown out the noise in my head. I was so cold. I shivered.

William further adjusted the covers in an attempt to block the air.

While he was standing beside me, holding my hand, the nursed knocked, entered again, and asked, "Kameleon, is there anything that we need to know about your medical history before we get started?"

"No ma'am," I replied.

"I see you noted on your form that you had one abortion before. Is that correct?"

"Yes ma'am," I said.

"When was that?"

"Four years ago," I said quietly.

"Okay, and are you two sure this is what you want to do?"

William and I looked at each other and nodded to the lady.

"Yes," I whispered, and William said it as well.

She patted my arm, left the room, and returned shortly after with the doctor.

"We're going to give you a little something to numb you from the waist down," the doctor said.

"Please turn on your right side."

William assisted me in turning to the right and I stared at the green wall while the nurse stuck a needle the length of a skewer in my back.

The anesthesia made my hips relax to the point that I could not feel anything from the waist down. As soon as I began to relax, I heard a machine start. It sounded a lot like a vacuum cleaner.

"Kameleon," the doctor said, "I need you to scoot your bottom down to the edge of the table and place your feet in the stirrups."

I scooted as best I could without any feeling.

"A little more, dear," he said.

I felt the pressure of something near my vaginal opening.

Because William was standing, he had a full view of what was happening. His eyes widened, which told me the procedure had begun.

With the specula in place, I could feel the pressure of the tube entering me. It was a little larger than a tampon. The suction sound grew louder as the pressure in my abdominal area increased. All of a sudden I heard a loud noise like a vacuum cleaner makes when it picks up a large object, or staple.

It felt like my insides were being suctioned out of me. I flinched and because I flinched William did as well.

I looked up at him and saw the sheer terror in his eyes. I was so wrapped up in the sounds that I had not had a chance to pay attention to my feelings.

This was impacting William as much as it was impacting me. I could tell that this experience was changing his outlook and perspective. He'd never witnessed anything like this before.

The fact that I could feel our unborn baby being torn from my body hurt me. And watching it hurt him.

I started to cry, first a few tears, then a stream of tears. *How am I in this situation again?* My experience four years ago was nothing like this. I had been put to sleep in the hospital so that I wouldn't remember any of it. Until now, I had not realized how traumatic the experience was. I didn't have a reference point. This day would be eternally etched in my mind.

The doctor turned the machine off. "We're all done honey. You can scoot back up on the table."

Realizing that feeling had returned to my lower extremities, I slowly inched my way back up the table. With another pat on my shoulder, the nurse left, following the doctor.

William and I remained, still as statues.

Through my tears I asked, "William, what have we done?"

He said nothing. There were no words.

We cried as we held each other. We knew what we had done was awful and could not be reversed. We realized how selfish we were.

February nineteenth was forever etched in our minds. We never spoke of that afternoon again.

OCTOBER 18, 1997

After Louis's death, Christian began to kick things into overdrive.

It was clear that the talk Louis had with him on his deathbed had a great impact on Christian. He was at home far more frequently than he had been in the past.

This made it difficult for me to carve out time to spend with William, although we still kept in touch.

It was clear that Christian was trying to put the pieces of his broken family back together. Still hurt from all the drama, I wasn't sure how I felt about all of the attention from Christian.

In the past I would have loved for our life to be like it was when we first got married and lived in the one-bedroom condo off of Snapfinger Woods. Back in those days, we didn't have much but we were happy. We would spend our Sundays on the sofa watching Lifetime movies all day.

Fast-forward- we barely saw each other or spent time with one another.

I was busy making a name for myself in the school district, and Christian was building his business and chasing dollar signs. It was hard to believe we were so far from where we started. I had settled into the married lifestyle enjoying be-ing *taken care of,* and Christian, despite his flaws and past is-sues clearly was focused on providing and keeping his family together. He began to invest heavily in the car business with his inheritance from his father, and he also began to grow his reputation and network within the car business.

Louis had left Christian and Braxton a lot of money, so this provided Christian with the opportunity to begin to live the life of his dreams. He had always loved cars and tried to model himself after my father in many ways.

After constant nagging and discussions, Daddy took Christian under his wing in order to teach him the wholesale car business. My father's business dealt primarily with used cars with names like Toyota, Honda, Ford and so forth.

Christian however was more interested in the so-called "highline" cars, Porsche, BMW, and the exotics. "The return on investment was far greater, and so was the demand, espe-cially here in the Atlanta area," he would tell me. "Here in Atlanta everyone, male and female, is flossing. Cars define your status," he said. "With all these ballers, recording artists, wannabe ballers and wannabe music moguls making Atlanta their home, there is plenty of money to be made. It's a shame, on any given day a man could be driving a Benz but living at his Mama and Daddy's house." Christian would add with a chuckle.

As a result of Christian's drive and work ethic, he began to differentiate himself in the market. People would seek him out whenever they were looking for a luxury vehicle at a good price. Money started to roll in, and Christian decided that it was time for him to part ways with my father and open his own lot that specialized in luxury vehicles.

He and his business partner Tim were *taking things to another level* from what my father had done. On any given day you would drive by our modest home and see a Bentley, a big body Benz or maybe even a Ferrari. The cars would attract all kinds of attention from our neighbors and Christian loved it.

I had been around cars my entire life so nothing he brought home excited me. Rather than having a traditional lot with cars out front, Tim and Christian opted to open an indoor lot, where their vehicles would be secure, and they began to crank out more units a month than the big names such as AutoNation and CarMax.

As a result of the close call, I had on the day of Louis's death, it had been a while since Kirby and I had hung out. With Christian being so attentive and needy, my block was hot and I found it difficult to get any time alone or to spend time with my friends. Since Christian was working late, and Ethan was with his Nana for the evening, I decided to meet Kirby for a few drinks at a cute little wine war called The Grape to catch up. Surprisingly, Kirby and I entered the parking lot at the same time.

"Hell must be about to freeze over, I can't believe you made it here on time," I said sarcastically as I jumped out the car.

Kirby and I both giggled as we hugged and walked inside.

"I was just finishing up a meeting up the street at the Red Cross so, I was in the area kind Ma'am," Kirby replied with a chuckle pretending to be defensive. "I miss you girl.

It seems like forever since we have seen each other," Kirby continued.

"Girl, my block has been hot. Christian is barely giving me any room to breathe. This is the most time he has spent with Ethan and me in a long time. He appears to be really *trying.* The only reason I am out tonight is because he had to work late and Ethan just happens to be hanging out with his Nana."

"Well, we did hang out all night the last time we were together. I can see why you might be under close observation and besides; he did just lose his father. That kind of loss can make anyone clingy. Louis and Christian were so close."

Christian and his father were close. I had not really taken the time to think about Christian's clinginess being as a result of losing Louis. I missed him dearly.

"So what have you been up to," I asked Kirby trying to get my mind off of Louis.

"Girl, nothing much. Just working really and trying to decide what the hell I am going to do about Algernon. "

Algernon was Kirby's longtime boyfriend that she was trying to figure out if she was going to keep or leave.

"He is still up to his same ole' bullshit. He won't decide what he is going to do with his life. I have practically given up on the Medical school thing and, just yesterday, he told me that his roommate of 3 years just got a job out of the country. The last time his roommate moved he lost his place and had to move in with me for a few months which turned into a few years. I am not doing that with him again."

"Oh, no Kirby. What are you going to do?"

"I am not going to do anything," Kirby snapped. "The question is, what is he going to do? But anyway girl, I don't even want to talk about that anymore, it's making me angry. What's going on with you and William?"

"I decided to pump the breaks with William. With all of the attention from Christian, I don't want to take the chance of getting caught up. We still talk and text occasionally but not much else. I have to admit Kirby, I miss him. More than the physical, there is an emotional connection that we share. He helped me through a very rough patch, where I was questioning everything from my looks to my confidence.

"You have no reason to question anything about yourself Kami. You're a beautiful woman. I just wish you would pay a little more attention to your heart than your pocketbook," Kirby said as she took a sip of her wine. I glanced up at her and could see the concern in her eyes. "Christian has put you through so much but, through it all you still stay. Why?"

I took a sip of my champagne and thought about Kirby's question. Why am I still here? Christian had cheated on me and taken me through hell. What was I afraid of? I had never been a needy or insecure woman. In fact, my self-concept had always been extremely high. What was I afraid of? Why had I allowed all of this to happen to me? Was I fighting for my marriage or trying to maintain my status quo? What did I really want?

Am I enough?

SEPTEMBER 27, 1993

*W*illiam was in town.

He had just finished summer training camp and was going to be playing his first preseason game with the Steelers against the Falcons here in Atlanta. The team hotel was situated on the outskirts of the city so as to provide the players with the least amount of distraction before kick-off.

"Meet me at the hotel after you finish classes," he'd said. "I can't leave the hotel, but we'll order in and watch movies."

I could imagine his grin was as big as mine at the thought.

At a near sprint, I entered my classroom in Giles Hall only to find that our professor had not arrived. I was twelve minutes late. It had taken everything in me to be disciplined and attend my classes today resisting my strong desire to skip my classes in lieu of lying up with William all day.

"Shit," I exclaimed upon entering the classroom and realizing we had no teacher. "I'm going to leave. He's late."

According to Spelman's attendance policy, if my Chaucer professor Dr. Nicks didn't arrive within the fifteen-minute grace period, class was automatically canceled for the day.

Once the classroom clock read twenty minutes after eleven AM, the rest of the class agreed with me, and as usual, we all finally opted to leave.

I was elated. This couldn't have happened on a better day because it meant I was finished for the day early, and William and I would have at least three hours together before he had to meet the team on the bus.

I stopped by my dorm room to grab my overnight bag, which was already packed, and bolted to the parking lot. *Thank you mom, for suggesting I schedule all my classes in the morning.*

The lobby of the hotel was conservatively decorated. Not at all what I would have expected from the NFL. I mean, the net worth of the people being housed between their walls was staggering. You would think they would have spent a little more to accommodate them. As I proceeded through the lobby toward the front desk, I giggled at the thought, I guess they had to save money somewhere.

William told me that he would leave a key at the front desk with my name on it and when I arrived, just to come on up. As a rookie, he didn't want to get caught by anyone on the coaching staff with his girlfriend in the lobby on the day of his first game but he knew he couldn't come to Atlanta and not at least spend a little time with me.

I approached a tall slender, pretty blonde standing behind a large mahogany and glass desk.

"Hi, I'm Kameleon Papillon here to see William Levy."

"Kameleon, yes, here you are. May I see your id please?"

I fumbled through my purse and quickly located my driver's

license and handed it to her. Smiling, she pushed a small envelope across the large desk. "I'm Abby should you need any assistance while you're here." She turned and pointed to her left. "The elevators are down the hall to your right. Please enjoy your stay."

I retrieved the envelope and felt the key card inside.

Butterflies fluttered in my stomach. *Boy did I love this man.*

I had seen William thousands of times but for some reason I was so nervous today.

It seemed like forever since we had seen each other and I was super excited to hear all about training camp.

I made my way to room 727, and stood for a moment outside the door. I could hear the faint sound of the TV and laughter in the background.

I inserted my key into the door and pushed it open trying to balance both my bag and the weight of the heavy door at the same time.

William was lying across the bed with his shirt off, facing the TV. He had his arm around a girl who was sporting only her bra.

"What's going on here," I asked, my voice cracking as tears of humiliation streamed down my face.

I stood frozen in the doorway, eyes burning at the sight before me.

My bag fell to the floor.

The laughter stopped.

William looked up at me like a deer in headlights. Clearly I was earlier than he'd expected. The girl grinned mischievously as she tried to place her arms around him.

I collected myself, grabbed my bag, and backed out of the room bolting in the direction of the elevator.

William broke free from her hold and jumped up running after me. "Kami," he cried out.

I ran and punched at the button to call the elevator.

"Kami," William called behind me.

An eternity later, the elevator doors opened and I scurried in, wiping away my hot tears as I faced the hall. He ran up to the doors, still fumbling with his pants, just as the doors closed to carry me down.

Tears streamed down my burning hot face. I was devastated. Why would he leave a key for me and allow me to walk into that? I asked myself as I ran out of the hotel sobbing uncontrollably. How could he be so careless and cruel?

OCTOBER 22, 2003

The administrative staff stayed until all of the parents and teachers were out of the building on parent-teacher conference nights, and tonight was no exception. The conferences had run long that evening, and it was close to ten at night when I finally made it home. As soon as I turned on to my street, I knew something was dreadfully wrong. The front door to my house was standing wide open. Sometimes when Ethan rode his bike, he would enter and exit out of the front door and forget to close the door tightly behind him. Maybe that was what happened, I thought, my stomach churning. Maybe the wind blew the door open.

As I got closer, I knew that wasn't the reason. My palms were sweating and my heart was beating in my ears. The door of the Benz that Christian had been driving all week was also standing wide open.

I gulped.

There were no other cars around. Our street was quiet. I pulled in the driveway behind the Benz, grabbed my work bag and purse, and ran to the door of my house. The minute

I stepped inside, my stomach lurched, and it was all I could do to keep from retching.

My house was a horror shop of destruction. Our Charles Bibb's pieces had been torn from the walls and sliced out of their frames. The stuffing from the sofa cushions was spread about like a mad winter blizzard and the glasses and plates from my china cabinet were shattered everywhere. There were deep gouges in the walls all over the living room. *What were they looking for?* I frantically ran from room to room screaming, calling, and looking for Ethan. After a few horrifying minutes, I heard his muffled cry. I sobbed. I was so shaken.

Christian and Ethan were gagged and tied together with plastic dog ties and propped against the bed in my bedroom. I screamed and ran to them crying as I tore at the bindings. Instinctively I went for Ethan first, clutching him to me while I kissed his forehead and rubbed his back.

With shaky hands I quickly untied them both.

"Oh my God Christian. What happened?"

"As I was getting Ethan out of the car, two men approached me and put a gun to my back. When I refused to unlock the door to the house, they kicked it in and ransacked the place, Kami," Christian said his voice trembling with fear. "I thought they were going to kill us. The safe is gone. They emptied your jewelry box. I'm sorry."

"It's okay," I reassured him, as he stood there, dazed, looking around. I comforted Ethan, who was still and stiff in my arms. "Look at me, Christian. For some reason this morning I decided to wear everything I have. I walked out looking like Mr. T."

"Thank God you did. You have something left, then," Christian said as he hugged Ethan and me.

"I'll call the police," Christian said, his voice firm. "You take care of Ethan."

I sat on the sofa, holding Ethan, soothing him, begging him to be okay, and asking him over and over how he felt, but Ethan remained stiff and silent in my arms.

Each time I asked him if he was ok, his eyes kind of glazed over and I imagined that his mind was going back to that horrible moment when the men came inside our home. I pulled Ethan to me in a tight embrace as Christian talked to the 911 operator and we waited for the police to arrive, the three of us all terrified and huddled together on what was left of our sofa in our damaged living room.

JUNE 3, 1994

"Kameleon darling, please be safe on the road," Mama said.

I was headed to Lafayette, Louisiana, the city in which I was born, and I was super excited. My parents, on the other hand, seemed depressed.

Dad looked over at her and then back at me. "Just be careful," he said. "You're the first to leave the nest."

"Daddy, I've made this drive with you so many times, I could do it blindfolded." I slammed the trunk door shut on my luggage. "And I didn't really leave the nest. I attended college in state, and you came to see me all the time."

"The last thing I need is for something to happen to you while you're going down there to see that man," Mama said. And when she said, "that man," she grimaced.

"So, that's what this is all about," I said.

They weren't concerned about the nine-plus hour drive that I had ahead of me. Instead, Mama and Daddy were concerned about the fact that I would be staying with my biological father and attending his wedding. Leave it to Mama to really put things out there. She never was good at biting her tongue. It was bad enough that they had kept me from him for the majority of my life.

"Look," I said. "I want to get to know him so I can understand where my personality comes from."

My Mama made a sound that I swear sounded like "harrumph."

She had always made it a point to tell me that I acted just like my father but, I didn't know him so I didn't know what the hell she was talking about when she said things like that. It would be good to finally know what she meant and who I was being compared to. I had seen pictures from when he and Mama were married, but for the most part I knew nothing about him. The only contact I had from him was when he came to see me one summer when I was visiting Auntie Mina and two years ago when an attorney reached out to my parents to let me know that his late Aunt Edna had left me a sizable inheritance from her estate. Apparently, my great Aunt Elsa and Edna were friends and she kept close tabs on my growth and progress during their monthly brunch. So, needless to say, when the executor of her estate reached out, I was shocked. I didn't even think anyone cared because no one had ever attempted to contact me prior to that, but that money helped to pay for a portion of my expenses while finishing up at Spelman.

Daddy came over to the driver's side window, slipped me a little more cash without Mama noticing and said, "Make sure you call me at every stop love."

"I will Daddy, love you, love you Mama," I yelled out the window as I backed out of the driveway. In my rear view mirror I could see the two of them holding each other and waving at me. I tooted the horn of my Geo Storm, blew a kiss at my parents, and headed down the street toward the expressway.

I couldn't drive through Baton Rouge without at least stopping to say hello to Auntie Mina. She knew I was on the road and besides being my favorite person in the world, her house made for an excellent resting point before I finished my trek on into Lafayette. Whenever my family would come off the road, Auntie Mina would have an amazing meal prepared for us and today was no different.

"Hi," Auntie Mina squealed as I entered her kitchen. She always made me feel so loved and so welcome.

"Hi," I squealed back as I ran to give her a huge hug. "I never get you all to myself. During Thanksgiving I have to share you with the rest of the family."

"Still haven't learned how to share I see," Auntie Mina said with a giggle as she kissed me on the forehead and ushered me inside.

It was times like this when it was just the two of us that I valued most of all.

"You hungry?" Auntie Mina asked.

"Starving. I snacked on the road because I didn't want to get sleepy, so it is definitely time to eat for real," I said.

Auntie Mina dished up two plates of crawfish etouffee and potato salad and poured two glasses of Chardonnay.

I plopped into a chair at the table and reached for my fork.

"You excited about your summer internship at the television station?" Auntie Mina asked.

"Kinda," I said. "It's a new market for me so I'm a little nervous. Lafayette, Louisiana is very different from the Atlanta University Center Broadcast I've been hosting for the past 2 years. Besides, it's bittersweet for me since this will be my last time in front of the cameras. I'm going to grad school in August to get my teaching certification."

"What?" Auntie Mina smiled. "That's great, but is it what you want?

"Mama and Daddy have really been working on me about career choices and they believe teaching is a more stable occupation."

"Kami, this is your career. You have to be happy with the life you choose. Your Mama and Daddy are living theirs. You have to live yours," Auntie Mina said, her voice and her face serious.

"I always thought I was going to be a teacher," I said. "I mean, I feel like I have been teaching all my life but, I do have to admit I loved my work as a reporter." I swirled my fork around in the bowl, thinking about how hard it had been to decide between the two careers.

"So what is it that you're nervous about? Seems like you've already made your decision in terms of career."

"I don't know, I really don't. And leave it to you to see that I'm nervous. I didn't even really realize that myself until you said it."

"Are you really nervous about the job or are you nervous because this is going to be the first time that you'll be spending time with your father?"

"Maybe a little of both."

Auntie Mina got up and hugged me. "Don't be nervous honey. He's going to love you and so is that television station.

I never shared this with you but, I know your father very well. He absolutely adores you. Before he and your mother broke up he would have you everywhere with him. You were, and still are, his pride and joy. Although he has taken a backseat to your Mama and Daddy, it doesn't mean he doesn't love or care about you."

I felt my cheeks redden as my eyes watered a little.

"There was a lot of confusion when your dad adopted you, especially when they decided to change your name. Your father was away in prison at the time and didn't see the posting in the newspaper in time to refute it. When he came home and realized what had been done, he was devastated. It sent him into an even darker downward spiral."

She sat back down and took my hand. "Give him a real chance this time Kami. More of a chance than you did the last time you saw him. You were so rude and angry then. Don't do that to him and don't do that to yourself. You need to know him. He is half of you and I truly believe that getting to know him will answer a lot of the questions you have about yourself."

I thought about how much I loved and respected this woman. I would walk on fiery coals for her so, if she said I needed to get to know my biological father, then I would, no questions asked.

"I'll be open to a relationship with him, Auntie Mina, I promise. I'll listen to what he has to say."

We moved on to other topics, and continued to talk, laugh, and drink our wine and before we knew it was after six p.m.

"Oh, Auntie Mina, since I don't really know where I'm going, I need to get back on the road before it gets too dark."

I helped her clear the table.

"Let these dishes go, Kami. You get on with the drive."

I kissed Auntie Mina and gave her a big hug. "Thank you for feeding me, and thank you for the advice. I promise I'll take it."

Lafayette was about an hour from Baton Rouge so, by the time I arrived it was close to seven thirty.

When I pulled up to the house, I could see my father standing in the window peering out.

Before I could get out of the car, he was at the door on the driver's side of my car, opening it to help me out.

Jordan Dean was a tall, dark, heavy set man standing about six foot two. Clearly I didn't get his height, I thought to myself.

His eyes were kind and his smile was infectious, just as I've been told that mine is. So many of my features had come from him, I thought, looking at him. My full pouty lips, high cheek bones, and slender chin were all courtesy of him.

"Welcome home honey," he said as he gave me a huge bear hug.

Auntie Mina had already broken down my shell, so I was able to relax into his hug and just allow it. Tears started rolling down my eyes. I wasn't even sure where they came from but they were flowing.

He grabbed my shoulders and pushed me back. "Let me look at you," he said.

I didn't want him to see me crying. I didn't want him to know that I was weak. He had to know that I was strong and that I was okay with or without him.

He took his finger and wiped the tears from my cheeks and said, "You will never be without me again until God calls me home and even then I will be watching over you," he said in an almost melodic tone. I batted my eyes a bit in an effort to stop the tears from flowing but eventually gave up. "I am so proud of you and your accomplishments," he continued. "I am so sorry that you had to grow up without me. I wasn't right when I was with your Mama, Kami. She didn't want you to be raised in that type of environment. She wanted better for you and for herself and I don't blame her at all for leaving. The drugs had me and no matter how hard I tried to fight them they always lured me back. I just couldn't beat them. I wasn't able to fully beat them until I found God." A single tear floated down his velvet cheek.

"After my last stint in prison, I vowed that I was going to make something out of my life. I knew that with the things I had done I would surely be dead if God didn't have a plan for me. A part of that plan is reconciling with you. My antics kept me away from you. Your parents didn't do that. You have every right to be angry with me not them. They did what they needed to do to protect and take care of you. It wasn't until I owned my truth that I was able to stop blaming others for the situation that I had created. I love you more than I love myself baby. I am willing to do whatever it takes to make our relationship how it should be, how God intended."

I wrapped my arms around his waist and hugged him tightly. The icebergs of my heart were thawing and in this single conversation, years of pain were melting away. Everything I had planned to say to him for so many years was out the window and, despite my inclination to be untrusting, the anger my heart had held for all these years was all of a sudden gone.

I chose to release it and in moments, it was replaced with an enormous amount of respect and love. He owned his truth and that was all I could ever ask for. I hugged him tightly. I felt him exhale and heard him let out a sigh. I could tell this moment was as emotional for him as it was for me. He hugged me back tightly and said, "Come, let's go inside, I want to introduce you to Katherine."

I can't stay here. Remembering what happened to you and Ethan here makes me cringe. Ethan still has nightmares."

"You're right, we need something much more secure," Christian agreed.

"Larger too," I said.

Christian had grown up in Southwest Atlanta, while I had grown up in Decatur. I was not fond of Southwest Atlanta, the area that many affectionately knew as the "SWATS"

We narrowed our list down and finally agreed on either Vinings or Sandy Springs, which put us in northern Atlanta.

During our first outing in Vinings we stumbled upon the perfect space. The house was located in a one street subdivision and had amazing views of the Atlanta skyline from the master bathroom tub.

"Christian, this place is absolutely perfect," I whispered trying to squelch the excitement that was bubbling inside of me. I jumped inside of the bathtub and laid back taking in the view of our amazing city.

"The closet is massive" Christian yelled from what seemed to be the other room. "I won't have to go into the guest bedroom to get dressed anymore," he said smugly. I giggled and thought to myself, shit you better hope you aren't sleeping in the guest bedroom.

My thoughts were interrupted by Christian's hand on my shoulder. "What do you think Kami? Should we put in an offer? I mean this is the first place we've looked at, there may be something better out there."

"Look at you, vintage Christian, always looking for the next best thing," I snarled back.

Christian recoiled with raised hands, "I'm just saying Kami. We've only seen this one house."

As much as I didn't want to agree, he was right. But, *this place was so perfect.* Maybe God was trying to make this process easy for us. Especially with all we had been through. "The last thing we need to do is make a hasty decision. We have to live here and this will probably be the last home we purchase. Our grand kids will visit us here. Let's take a minute and think it over" I said as I peeled myself out of the huge footed soaking tub.

We thanked the agent for her time, told her we would be in touch and headed to our car. "Something tells me that we should at least put in an offer and tie up this place," Christian said as we pulled off of the street. "We can always back out before it goes under contract if we find something better." I agreed. Christian fumbled in his pocket pulling out the agent's business card. He handed the card to me and I dialed the number and placed the phone on speaker. The agent answered on the first ring. "Hi this is Christian Beck. My wife and I just left a minute ago from touring the house.

"Oh yes Mr. Beck, how may I help you sir?"

"We would like to put in an offer on the home."

"I'm sorry sir, I hate to tell you this but a couple toured the house an hour before you and your wife. They called just as you two were leaving and put in a full price offer. The house is now under contract." My heart sunk to my stomach. "What. That quickly," Christian asked in utter amazement.

"I'm sorry sir but unfortunately yes, that quickly. We have a few other homes in our other subdivision that might interest you."

Disappointed, Christian replied, "Ok email the addresses to me and we will check them out. Thank you." I clicked end. I was in complete shock.

A few weeks later, after my hair appointment with Erin, I decided to look around a bit to see what Sandy Springs was like and to see if there was anything that remotely compared to what we had just missed out on. I still couldn't believe that before we were able to put in an offer the house had been snatched up. I was so disappointed. It was perfect and we needed to get out of our house in Stone Mountain in the worst way. Ethan was having terrible nightmares and Christian now slept with his gun. I had been on pins and needles for years since I caught that crazy bitch watching me through my window.

I turned left on Johnson's Ferry Road and stumbled upon another tiny one street subdivision that appeared to be still under development. I turned in and was simply in awe of the homes. There was no way Christian and I could afford one of these. They were gorgeous. About halfway down the street, I came upon one with a for sale sign in the front of it. I slowly pulled up the driveway and hopped out to peek in the window of the front door. The house had an amazing entry with a spiral-arched staircase that was to die for. I quickly called the number on the sign to see if the agent could meet me and show me the home. Mr. Sanford immediately answered. "Hi, Mr. Sanford, this is Kameleon Beck. How are you today sir?"

"Call me Charles," a cheerful southern voice replied.

"Ok Charles," I said with a chuckle and a smile. "I'm calling you about the home located at 177 Windsor Cove."

"Yes Ma'am, she's a beauty isn't she?"

"Yes she is Charles, is she available?"

"Why, yes Ma'am she is. Would you like to see her?"

"Yes sir. In fact, I am standing on the front porch right now. Can you meet me here?"

"I can but it will be around 6 before I can be there. Will that work for you?"

I looked at my watch; it was already 5:30 p.m.

"Yes, Charles, that works perfectly."

"Ok, well in the meantime, if you go around to the side of the house you will see the air conditioning units. Reach around to the back right. Back there, you will find a metal key holder. The key to the front door is inside. Why don't you go inside and have a gander and I will see you in just a few minutes."

Elated I said, "Oh, thank you Charles. See you in a minute."

I quickly hung up the phone and ran to retrieve the key. Upon entrance, the home enveloped me absolutely taking my breath away with its white washed cabinets, Juliette balconies and soaring ceilings. The style of this house was more traditional but still gorgeous in it's own right. I called Christian and told him that he had to meet me there pronto. He was playing golf so, he was less than excited about hurrying through his last few holes but knew better than to tell me no.

I locked myself inside the house and waited for Christian to arrive. I was afraid to leave because of the experience we had with the other house in Vinings. By this time, it was close to 6 which meant that Christian and Mr. Sanford would be arriving soon. So, I sat on the floor in the master bedroom and waited for them to get there. Christian arrived first and was as taken away with the home as I was. Although it was more expensive than the one in Vinings, no price could be put on our safety. When Mr. Sanford arrived, we placed a full price offer and our new home went under contract that day. Charles commented, "Well that was my easiest sell ever. Maybe I should not be around more often." We all chuckled. Our closing was scheduled for November twenty-eighth, which would get us into our dream home right before the Christmas holidays. I was ecstatic and quickly began to make preparations for both the move and Christmas with the family in our new home.

AUGUST 20, 1994

After two wonderful months in Lafayette with my dad and Katherine, it was hard to believe I was back in Atlanta.

His wedding to Katherine, a tall, cinnamon-colored lady, was perhaps the sweetest ceremony I had ever witnessed. In their living room, surrounded by immediate family, which consisted of me, Katherine's two children, her sisters, mom and my father's brothers, they exchanged their self-composed vows. It was clear that she loved my father deeply and that he was in love with her. She had helped him to turn his life around and develop a relationship with God. Apparently, they had dated before he met my mom and she was heartbroken when she found out that he had married another woman. Thankfully their love had come full circle and now they would be able to spend the rest of their lives together.

Katherine was the nicest person I had ever met. She was so attentive and easy to talk to. Many evenings after dinner, we would sit on the sofa and share stories. Katherine wanted to know everything about me and because she was so amazing,

I wanted to learn more about her. She made me feel so comfortable and welcome that when it was time for me to return to Atlanta, it was hard for me to leave.

She and my father both cried this morning as we loaded my car. "You know I'd planned to stay through the weekend, but I can't pass up Niki's wedding. Although the wedding is a bit of a surprise, she would never forgive me."

Niki was a close family friend, my Godparents' daughter. Our families had moved to Atlanta together years ago from Baton Rouge to open a car dealership.

"We are just going to miss you so much love," Katherine said.

"Yea, I wish you could stay forever," my father added.

It had been an amazing summer full of new experiences with my father and stepmother. By the end of my visit, all of my questions had been answered, and I felt solid on where my relationship with he and Katherine was headed. I waved and blew each of them a kiss as I pulled out of the driveway and headed back to Atlanta for the evening ceremony.

After the wedding reception, the bride and groom threw an after party for the younger guests at Tongue and Groove, one of Atlanta's top-rated clubs. As I was standing outside of the club waiting to get in, I spotted Christian Beck and his best friend Gill exiting the club. It had been years since we had seen each other so I doubted that he would recognize me.

Unlike some of the guys I crushed on when I was young, Christian had aged well. He was still incredibly handsome, and with his coal black wavy hair and dark features he was hard to ignore. Gill spotted me looking at them and whispered something to Christian. Christian spotted Moni and I sitting on a bench outside the door of the club and headed over with Gill in tow, both with huge smiles on their faces. I braced myself for what was sure to be a spectacle as Christian approached me with outstretched arms. "Kami, how've you been girl," Christian exclaimed.

Before I knew it, he had scooped me up and was spinning me around in the air like a rag doll.

"Christian, put me down," I demanded as I beat him in the back until he placed me back down safely on the ground. Gill and Moni were in full giggle as I tried to regain my composure.

"What the hell happened to a regular hello, Christian?" I yelled as I tried to steady myself from the dizzying escapade I had just experienced.

Forever the charmer, Christian replied, "Regular hello's are for regular girls. You're by no means regular, Kameleon Papillon."

"Oh lawd. " Gill sighed. "Here we go."

We all giggled as Christian stood there red-faced as if he didn't know what was going on.

"What's so funny," Christian asked.

We all continued to laugh.

"Save the lines Christian, those are for regular girls," I said. "You always were a charmer."

"You avoided me when we were younger, Kami, but I'm not about to allow that to happen again." Christian's tone had gone from playful to serious in a matter of a few seconds.

Noticing the change in atmosphere, Moni and Gill stepped over to the side so that Christian and I could talk.

"Listen Christian," I said. "Our party is about to move inside but let's exchange numbers. I would love for us to hang out sometime and catch up."

Christian grinned when I handed him my phone and allowed him to dial his number from it.

"Now, we're connected again," I said. "See, that wasn't so bad, was it?" I smiled at him. His hand lingered for a moment on mine as he passed back my phone.

Christian smiled back and then leaned over to kiss me on my cheek. He whispered, "I'll call you tomorrow."

I nodded, collected Moni, who was being held hostage by Gill, and we walked into the club.

NOVEMBER 30, 2003

Why was someone calling us on the house phone? Everyone close to us knew that this was move-in weekend.

Christian and Ethan were at the new house sorting boxes and placing them in the appropriate rooms while I retrieved some final items from the old house and said goodbye to the Hogans.

The Hogans had been the first people to welcome Christian and I to the neighborhood. We had grown quite close to them over the last seven years and I wanted to drop off a bottle of wine for old times' sake.

I placed the box that I was carrying on the floor next to the door leading to the garage and grabbed the phone. "Hello," I said.

"Hi, may I speak to Mr. Christian," a small voice said.

"Christian is not in. May I ask who is calling?"

"This is Michael."

"Well hello Michael, can I help you with something?"

"Can you ask Mr. Christian to bring some batteries over when he comes to our house?"

"I don't understand, Michael. Why would Mr. Christian be bringing batteries to your house?"

"Because he always brings what we need to the house. He's my mom's boyfriend, and she said we can ask him for whatever we need. That he's got money and he likes to spend it on us."

"Is that so?" My voice took on a high-pitched, tense sound, even to my own ears. "And what's your mom's name Michael?"

"Dominique." The small voice sounded a little unsure.

"Okay, Michael, I'll be sure to let Mr. Christian know that you called."

"Oh, thank you."

"You're very welcome dear."

I hung up and stumbled to a chair. *I am so dumb.*

I glanced around at the boxes, remnants of our life together here in this house. I thought about the times we'd spent laughing, crying, shouting at each other, and loving each other.

How was he able to continue to do this to me?

Just when I was beginning to relax back into our relationship, and thought he was reformed, this shit happens. We had just closed on our dream home, for God's sake. Here I was, stupidly thinking that maybe this could be a new start for us; that we could put everything that had happened in our relationship behind us. Perhaps even have another child and continue to build our family. Why did he continue to build with me when he obviously didn't want to be married to me? What was my purpose in his life? Was it all about the material things that we had acquired together? Was I just a stepping-stone? A means to an end?

I was torn between my anger, my fears for the future, and heartache.

We were building a small empire together? Wait, I got him into the car business. It was my family connections that helped him climb the ladder to become the top grossing used car broker in the state. We were a force to be reckoned with-Christian making a name for himself in the car business and me making a name for myself in education.

A tear slid down my cheek, then another one.

I had been happy; happier and more peaceful than I had been in years. After Louis's death I vowed to try to forgive and put the past behind me for the sake of my marriage. I had just been selected as the first female and first African-American principal of one of the most prestigious schools in the state at the ripe age of thirty-five. To most, we appeared to have it all. I actually did think we had it all.

Boy was I wrong. Our marriage was fucked up. After eight years, we still couldn't figure it out.

My breath quickened as I slid down the wall and sat down on the floor. My tears flowed, but I could feel the anger just under the surface. I realized that it had always been about Christian achieving his goals. He wanted to change me into some kind of flawless wife. He never once really looked at me for who I was. He wanted me to be someone else. I was by no means perfect, but then again, obviously, neither was he.

Christian clearly had decided to live a separate life while maintaining his current one.

What was I going to do? I was not about to let someone capitalize on what I had built, especially after all I had been through.

Sitting on the kitchen floor in my old house, I wiped my tears and decided not to make a big deal out of this incident. Christian was a liar and cheater and that was not going to change. Besides, what exactly would I be fighting for? There was nothing left in our marriage. Would I be fighting for the house? The cars? The money? Hell, my attorney would get all of that if I decided to divorce him.

This information would be much better served tucked away as further justification for my own past transgressions. I just hoped Michael wouldn't spill the beans.

MAY 13, 1995

Not a day goes by that I don't see or hear from Christian. It is almost as if we are in some kind of time warp because every moment is spent either thinking about each other or spending time with each other.

I pulled up to Christian's father's house and as usual Louis was sitting on his porch excited to see me.

"Hey Kami," he called out. "How's it going today?"

"Just fine sir, how are you?"

"I can't complain for an ole' man."

We giggled. "Where's Christian?"

He grinned and pointed. "He's inside. Go on upstairs and see what you can find."

I left Louis outside on his porch in his rocking chair as he always was, with his glass of red wine in his hand, and I headed upstairs to find Christian. Although he had aged, he was still handsome as ever. A true silver fox. I loved that old man because he always had a way of making me smile even on my worst days.

When I walked into Christian's room, he was folding clothes.

He saw me and began to smile, a smile that went from ear to ear.

I went over and gave him a hug and a kiss on the ball of his cheek as I always did. Then, I sat on the edge of the bed and began to help him finish folding the small mountain that had accumulated.

"Thanks for helping me out with the laundry. I don't know where all those clothes came from," he said with a giggle as we put the last of them away.

I rolled my eyes at him and said sarcastically, "I know where they came from. You take umpteen showers a day." With a smirk on my face, pleased with my comment, I bolted for the doorway and through the hall headed for the stairs as Christian chased me. Giggling, I flew passed the huge picture windows and finally let him catch me. "It's a beautiful day. We shouldn't spend it inside. Wanna go to the park?"

"Sounds like a plan." Christian said. "Go get a blanket from upstairs and I'm going to steal a bottle of wine and some glasses."

"Don't forget candles," I yelled as I grabbed a blanket from the hallway closet and picked up the boom box from Christian's room on my way back downstairs.

As we were leaving, Louis said with a laugh, "Lord have mercy. I'm being robbed."

We all giggled.

"Hey you guys, don't be alarmed if I'm not here when you get back this evening. I have a hot date." He said as he stroked the smooth gray hairs of his beard.

"You're going to hang out with Samantha, aren't you, old man?" Christian laughed.

"Maybe I am and maybe I'm not," he responded coyly. "Mind your own business young'n," he concluded with a chuckle.

We always wondered why Louis never cemented his relationship with Sam. Maybe it was because Sam was white. Although none of us kids cared about that, Velma would have had a conniption. Still today, when they are in a room together, the atmosphere is tense despite the fact that they have been divorced for God knows how long. Christian once shared with me that Louis had cheated on Velma with a white woman and Velma was never able to forgive him for it. After years of trying to work things out, she divorced Louis and eventually remarried years later. Louis however, had chosen to remain a bachelor even though it was clear that he loved Sam and she adored him. Louis thought that no one knew how close he and Sam had become, but truly, everyone knew.

Christian and I eyed each other and smiled at the news that Louis was not going to be home when we returned.

"You think he told us on purpose?" I asked Christian.

"Probably so. He is cool like that," Christian responded.

It meant that we would have a little bit of alone time. Since both Christian and I were still staying at home with our parents, it was difficult for us to capture those small moments.

"Let's fix dinner once we return from the park and then maybe jump into the Jacuzzi," Christian said.

I always enjoyed spending time in the Jacuzzi. It helped to relax my tired muscles and Christian would always jump at any opportunity to get me in my birthday suit.

I smiled at him.

When we arrived at Piedmont Park, we saw that the area where we normally laid out to people watch was occupied by a family and their two dogs.

"It's so crowded here," I said.

"How about down here," Christian said, leading me to a place a little further down, close to the lake.

Once we got our spot all situated and the music playing, we sat there in silence for a bit. It felt good, taking in the scenery and enjoying the quiet stillness of the day. A butterfly had taken a liking to the hydrangea bushes in front of us. I watched it as it gracefully flitted from bloom to bloom until it finally landed on the most spectacular one of all. What was it about that particular bloom that beckoned it to stay? Why that bloom at that moment?

"Do you realize we've seen each other every day since August twentieth?"

"Yes," I responded still distracted by the antics of the butterfly on the hydrangea bloom. "I was just thinking about that today when I pulled up to your house."

"I really enjoy our time together," Christian said. "When I saw you back in August I never thought that this would lead to something quite like this. Everything has been so easy breezy, I mean, we just flow. I want to spend time with you. There's no pressure for anything more than a friendship and I think that's what makes me love you more. Now, I can't imagine my life without you in it."

I waited a moment, letting Christian's words sink in. It was true that our relationship had evolved organically in a very short period of time. The more time we spent together. The more difficult it became for us not to be with each other. I had grown to look forward to our time together. I had been on a self-proclaimed relationship vacation until Christian and I were reunited. He was a welcomed diversion from thoughts of my failed relationship with William.

Since graduating from Spelman, my Mama and Daddy had become increasingly more demanding. Well, not really my Daddy, mostly my Mama. She was constantly encouraging me to push forward with additional degrees.

"You know," I said. "I look forward to our time together too. I feel relaxed with you. At home, my parents are always pushing me."

I watched as the butterfly flitted away.

"Daddy's thing is he wants me to commit to a career in education and perhaps be one of the district superintendents in our state. It's almost too much. I have absolutely no desire to be a superintendent of any school district and I feel like because neither of them graduated from college, they're living vicariously through me."

"You don't want to be a teacher?" Christian reached out to touch my shoulder gently.

"Don't get me wrong," I said. "I believe that the teaching profession is one of the noblest professions out there, but after this first year of grad school, I feel like I have more to give and my purpose is far greater."

"I think I understand," he said. "You want more out of life."

"I often played school as a child and stayed after school with my teachers, collecting all of the old materials and supplies so that I could have a fully stocked classroom at home," I said. "But all that time, I watched my teachers taking care of other people's bad ass children, and I wanted more out of my life than that. I always saw myself as someone who would do more than just teach others." I sighed. "Creativity is bubbling inside of me and my interests are all over the place, but mostly in arts and entertainment. My parents are not going to have that. I can hear my Mama saying, 'I didn't send you to

Spelman for you to become a starving artist. Your Dad and I have invested too much money in your education for you not to use it' like she says a lot."

Christian laughed, and so did I.

"I've conformed to the ideal they have in their minds for what my future will look like. And I continue to press forward in my graduate program. But, to nurture my creative side, I maintain my manager-in-training position at Talbots."

Christian was silent for a few minutes, just touching me, rubbing my shoulder.

I knew he was also struggling to find his way. A former college athlete, he had been sent to school on a track scholarship and was now forced to figure things out outside of sports. It was clear that his track career was over and he needed to find out where his passion was. For the time being, he was working at FA Rent-all as a delivery manager.

"You know," Christian said, "When I started that job at FA Rent-all, I thought I would be managing the logistics associated with customer deliveries but I was horrified to find out that delivery manager meant I'm actually the person delivering the appliances or furniture. I didn't see myself using my college degree to deliver furniture."

Apart we were weak, but together we were strong and able to accomplish more. Although neither of us was where we wanted to be, we were both further along than most of the people that we knew. We both had jobs that brought in a considerable amount of money for new college graduates. Between the two of us we made about $50,000 a year, which was more than most people our age were making at that time.

I leaned over and kissed Christian on his cheek. "We are really good for each other," I replied.

Christian glanced at me with a crooked smile and said, "Forever the cool one, let me in, Kami," Christian said.

"I'm not being cool, I'm being cautious," I said. "Look, I have been betrayed a lot in my young life. Pardon me if I am a little timid when it comes to commitment and relationships."

"You can't judge me based on what others have done Kami. I'm different. Our relationship is different and you know that," Christian said. "I have known you since you were four years old. Our families attend the same church. I knew when I started dating you that I had to be real with you. That this relationship was nothing to play with."

"I understand, Christian, and I appreciate your passion and commitment to us. It means the world to me. Let's just enjoy each other and our time together."

With that, Christian laid back on the blanket and I laid in his lap. I took some time to finally finish *The Bluest Eye* by Toni Morrison while Christian cat napped in the sun for the rest of the afternoon.

The stars began to peek through indicating night was near. Famished, we packed up our park gear and left. Thankfully, we'd gone grocery shopping yesterday and had some steaks marinating. All we had to do was throw them on the grill and make a salad and dinner would be ready.

As soon as we hit the door to the house, Christian went outside to light the grill and turn the Jacuzzi on while I began to prepare the salad and get the meat tray ready. By the time he made it back to the kitchen from lighting the grill, the tray was ready and I was passing it to him hurriedly so that he could get started.

Before he left the kitchen to tend to his grilling duties, he planted a wet kiss on the back of my neck and retreated before I could catch him.

I smiled and went back to dicing the veggies for our salad.

We sat on the deck enjoying the cool evening breeze and an amazing meal. It was so pretty out there.

Christian was quiet and kind of fidgety for the majority of our meal.

I wondered if he was still thinking about our park conversation so I asked, "Babe, what's wrong? You have been kind of quiet since we have been home. Is everything ok?"

"I have something to ask you Kameleon," Christian said.

"Anything honey, what is it?"

"Remember earlier today when I told you that I could not imagine my life without you in it?"

"Yes, I remember."

Christian slowly got up out of his chair and knelt before me.

My heart raced as I watched him pull a tiny box out of his pocket. Was this really happening? Was he about to do what I was thinking? Surely not. We had only been dating six months. How could he be so sure? How did he know I was the one for him?

Christian opened the box and inside sat a diamond band. "Will you marry me Kameleon?"

I was speechless. I am not even sure whether I answered his question or not. Wasn't this every little girl's dream? To one day have a husband to love and care for her?

But there I was, sitting there dumbfounded. I couldn't figure out what to say or do next. I looked in Christian's eyes and thought again about his proposal and considered how my life would change. I would be free to spread my wings, live on my own terms, and be out of my parents' grasp. My parents were great people who supported me in everything I have ever done, but after living alone on campus, it was difficult to come back to their house and their rules.

If I married Christian, that would be over. Just as Christian was about to stand and retreat I said in a soft voice, "Yes."

Christian's once sad eyes danced with excitement as he scooped me up into his arms like a mother cradles a baby and spun me around in circles. "I promise to love and take care of you baby," Christian said. "I promise I will."

DECEMBER 25, 2003

This Christmas by Donny Hathaway blasted throughout the house as we buzzed around putting the finishing touches on what was to be an epic Christmas feast.

Lynie was floating around the kitchen and family room still beaming from Colin's morning marriage proposal and Mama and Daddy were tag teaming, as they normally did, in an effort to complete the final dishes. My pristine new kitchen seemed to be holding its own.

Christian and I were preparing Christmas cocktails. Our family was helping us to break in our new home by celebrating Christmas in it this year, and the normal energy and holiday cheer was ever-present.

Mama, Daddy, Lynie, her now fiancé Colin, and my nephew Colin Jr., all had spent the night with us on Christmas Eve so that we could wake up together on Christmas Day as we had for all almost all our lives. Our home was large enough for everyone to have his or her own bedrooms and bathrooms and I had spent the past month making sure every room was furnished and ready for the holidays. The only person that was missing was Dia. We had no idea where she was. Since she started doing music, she hardly ever made it to family functions anymore but she never missed Christmas so we knew she would show up sooner or later.

Just as Mama and Daddy put the last dish on the banquet table, Dia came busting through the front door dressed in Goth, and ever ready to start some shit. She just couldn't be peaceful.

"How y'all gon start Christmas dinner without me," she asked?

"Dia darling, no one was going to start without you and Merry Christmas to you as well young lady," Mama replied.

Daddy didn't say a word. He just looked at her with his crooked grin as he always did, just happy to have all of his girls in the same place at the same time.

But everyone else saw that Dia looked a hot mess. Her thick black eyeliner had run halfway down her face and her clothes looked as if she had been wearing them for days. It was clear that she had been out all night. No one in their right mind would have intentionally walked out of the house looking like that. Judging from her tone and the way she swayed from side to side it was clear that she was under some type of influence.

When Dia was younger we used to think that she was just odd. I'll never forget the time when Lynie and I were playing "Superbaby" on the floor while watching cartoons. I loved playing Superbaby with Lynie. I would lie on my back with my feet in the air balancing Lynie on top of them. Once she was up in the air, she would let out these deep guttural laughs as she flew high above my head. Lynie was about two at the time, which meant that Dia could not have been more than six months old. When Lynie and I had completed our final landing we looked over and Dia had climbed all the way to the top of the bookshelf and was sitting there laughing and watching us from her perch. Lynie and I both screamed in unison for Mama to come and get her down.

"Y'all all drinking and happy and ain't nobody called me" Dia said, her face in a pout.

Her tone and the way she curled her lip reminded me of Auntie Stevie, which could only mean one thing. Did this shit run in the family?

Christian, noticing my confusion and concern, called me into the foyer so that we could speak in private.

"Kami," he said in a serious tone. "Word on the street is that Dia has been doing a little more than drinking. I keep hearing rumors about your sister and her drug use."

I felt weak. I looked back into the room where Dia was still talking loudly.

"Judging from the way she's looking today, I believe it's true and obviously getting progressively worse. We need to do something about it before she gets herself into more trouble."

"Oh, Dia," was all I could say.

"I know. I didn't want to share this with you but Gill called me last week after picking her up from some party at a hotel. He said, and I'm not sure if this is true or not Kami, but he said that there were condoms all over the place and he believed that several men had run a train on her." I gasped and held my face in my hands. "I have some friends that are some not-so-nice people. I can have them take care of her source but we need to take care of her."

"What do we do, Christian?" I asked. "Do we tell Mama and Daddy?"

"We need to do whatever we can to keep her out of the streets."

I shook my head in agreement. "I'll talk with Mama, Daddy, and Lynie." Still disgusted from the visual of the scene Christian had described in the hotel room, I followed him back to the family, now in the dining room for the blessing and dinner.

As I sat down to eat my meal, I couldn't get the conversation out of my mind. *Who the hell did he know?* He wasn't a part of that kind of lifestyle. How could he handle this? My thoughts slowly faded as I tried to settle back into the conversation with my family to enjoy the rest of my meal and Christmas holiday.

AUGUST 17, 1995

*W*ho could be calling me from a four seven zero area code? What state was that anyway?

With all the moving parts to this day, I just couldn't seem to keep up. Thank goodness for Moni. She had taken the day off from the law firm where she was interning to help me out.

This Saturday was the big day. The day I was to marry Christian. I still had a slew of things to complete before I got on that plane for Louisiana tomorrow.

By the third call from the unknown phone number I was growing impatient and tired of sending the persistent caller to voicemail.

"Hello," I answered, annoyed and short.

"What's up Kami Kam?"

I knew that voice anywhere. It was William Levy.

I wanted to say, "What the hell do you want," but instead I was silent while I gathered my thoughts. Why was he calling me today of all days?

"Hi William, what's up? Mighty fine hearing from you."

"Long time no speak," William responded.

"How is the NFL treating you?"

"Aww, I can't complain," William said. "How is grad school?"

"It's perfect. William, I know you didn't call me out of the blue for small talk, what's up?"

There was a momentary silence on the line and then William asked, "Are you getting married Kami?" *How the hell did he find out?* "My boy Maceo called me and told me that he heard that you were engaged."

In total disbelief, I replied, "Yes William I am engaged. In fact, the wedding is this Saturday."

There was another long silence on the phone. So long that I thought the call had disconnected.

In a shaky voice, William asked, "Were you not going to call and tell me Kami? I mean we dated for three years and almost had a child together. You don't think I at least deserved to hear this information from you? I had to hear about your wedding on the street."

"William, I didn't think you cared and I don't owe you anything. I haven't heard from you since the day I walked out of your hotel room; the hotel room that you were in with another woman after you invited me there to spend time with you."

"Kami, you never let me explain and refused to take my calls. What was I supposed to do?"

"William, how were you going to explain that? What could you possibly say to me to make that entire situation ok? Never mind. Don't even try to answer that- It's all good."

There was another long silence on the line.

"Why do you have to do this now? Are you ready for marriage Kami? You're such a free spirit and always talked about living on your own for a bit after school. What changed? Why the rush?"

William was right. When I was younger, I had dreamed of being rich and famous. I was never sure for what or how, but I wanted to touch people all over the world in some way; perhaps a clothing designer, entertainer, or journalist who traveled the world reporting on major events. Instead, I was now enrolled in grad school studying to be a teacher. That's a far cry from the career I had always envisioned myself to have.

What had changed? Why was I settling?

"Look William," I said, "I love Christian. That's what changed."

"Does love mean you can't go after your own dreams?"

I grew increasingly uncomfortable with the conversation and William's probing. Finally I asked, "Why do you care? You're living your dreams. You weren't worried about me before you heard I was getting married. Why are you acting like you're so concerned now?"

"I am concerned, Kami, because I love you and I only want what's best for you. I don't think this is best for you. I think you're settling."

Did he just use the same word I had thought a few moments before? I became even more agitated.

"William, I appreciate your call and the kind gesture, but I can't do this with you. I'm getting married Saturday for God's sake. This conversation should have happened way before now. I have to go. Please take care of yourself."

As I lowered the phone from my ear I could hear William trying to say something, but I hung up before I could make out the words. Thank goodness he did not call back.

I had to admit our conversation had left me shaken. Why do niggas wait until you can't breathe to profess how much they care? William had me doubting everything. Thoughts I had pushed to the back of my mind long ago were resurfacing.

With trembling hands, I picked up the phone and dialed Moni and Kirby on three-way. Surprisingly, they both answered.

"I can't do this," I said to them through spitty sobs.

"Can't do what," Kirby asked.

"I can't marry Christian Saturday."

"Kami, what do you mean you can't marry Christian?"

"I'm not ready for marriage. What was I thinking? It's not right." I was gasping by this time.

"You've been so sure all along. Did something happen," Moni said.

I paused for a minute trying to regain my composure and said, "William just called."

There was a pregnant pause and then Kirby said, "Kami, what the hell? I know you're not going to let that man drag you through anything else. Do remember how that relationship ended? Do you want that again? William broke your heart and here he is again ironically showing up in your life two days before you marry Christian." She paused.

"Oh you're getting married on Saturday, Kameleon Papillon. I already bought my dress and my plane ticket," Moni said. "If I have to drag you, you're getting on that plane."

Kirby and Moni were right. Where had William been for the past year? I hadn't spoken to him since I left his hotel room that day. All of the preparations had been made and my parents had spent a ton of money on this wedding. I wanted something small but they insisted on going all out since

I was the first of their daughters and the first grandchild to get married. I am perhaps the only one that my grandfather would get to see walk down the aisle. He had recently been diagnosed with cancer of the bone marrow and had not been given much time to live.

My Auntie Mina had been planning for months to ensure that everything was perfect. I just couldn't disappoint everyone. Because my mother knew me and had a feeling that something like this might go down, she had asked Moni to fly in at the same time as me to ensure that I made it to Baton Rouge for my wedding on time.

Now, Moni and Kirby decided that it would be best that Moni spend the night at my parents' house with me and we ride into the airport together, even though, her parents' house was the closest to the airport.

My friends weren't taking any chances.

"I'm already packed," Moni said. "So, after I pick up your lingerie, I will head your way."

The next morning Moni made sure that we were at our departure gate thirty minutes before our boarding time, so when the gate agent began to board the plane, we were two of the first onboard.

A pretty, older white flight attendant approached us and asked, "Can I get either of you ladies something to drink."

I glanced at Moni and then replied to the flight attendant, "Scotch and soda." Never mind the fact that it was just eight in the morning. By the time we landed in Baton Rouge I was lit. It didn't matter where they took me or what they asked me to do, everything was *all good.*

AUGUST 19, 1995

Three 1932 black Duesenbergs pulled up to Auntie Mina's house to transport us to my great Aunt Elsa's house.

She lived up the street from the church where the ceremony was to take place. It was decided her house would be the best place for the bridal party to get dressed and take family pictures. Since I had a near breakdown a couple of days prior, my girls had decided to forgo the bachelorette party they had planned for a more quiet evening of cocktails and conversation. They didn't want to take any chances with me being unprepared for my big day.

Aunt Elsa was outside in her driveway talking to her neighbor Bertha when we pulled up. She had told everyone on her street about the wedding so when our cars pulled up, all of her nosey neighbors had found some reason to be outside on their front porches sweeping, drinking coffee, or just outright staring.

Aunt Elsa spotted us and quickly ran to the side of the car with her hands wagging in the air while screaming broken

French phrases. "Well hello Miss Kami," she said as she opened the car door. "Are you ready for your big day?"

I smiled at her obvious good spirits "As ready as I'm going to be."

"Let me help you with your things darling." Aunt Elsa went to the back of the Duesenberg as the rest of my family pulled up.

Any time we were all together it was a reason to party, so Aunt Elsa had her usual snacks and champagne waiting on us when we entered her home. The champagne definitely took the edge off as I began to settle into the fact that within the next four hours I was going to be married to Christian.

My sisters brought in the dresses while my mother and Auntie Mina led the makeup artist to my dressing room.

Between the soft jazz that was playing in the background and the glass of champagne I was sipping, I began to relax. It was good to have my family around me and if nothing else, I felt loved. I waited patiently as the makeup artist set up all of her supplies. I was a little concerned that I would be overdone, since I didn't wear much makeup. However, I had long since realized that today really wasn't about me. Today was about my mother and Auntie Mina.

If it had been left up to me, Christian and I would have gotten married in Vegas in a tiny ceremony surrounded by close family and friends. Instead, half of Atlanta and all of Baton Rouge were preparing for what would be one of the most talked-about weddings of the year.

"I'm ready for you, Kami," the makeup artist said, motioning to a chair.

I said, "Typically I don't wear much makeup. If you could just give me a golden glow that'd be fine."

"Oh, no darling," she said. "You're going to have to have more than just a golden glow so that your face will show up in your pictures. I promise I won't do too much, and I promise you'll love it."

With that, I smiled at her, and settled into the seat and allowed her to do her magic.

Before I knew it, she was done.

She turned me around to face the mirror and I smiled.

She had done an amazing job. It wasn't too much and it wasn't too little. It was perfect.

My mother and Auntie Mina couldn't wait any longer and they busted into the room.

"Oh my goodness," Auntie Mina said with a squeal. You look beautiful Kami."

Mama was speechless and started crying at the sight of me.

"Mama don't cry. You're going to make me cry and then I'm going to smear the eyeliner that this kind lady just applied." I said as I hugged her and handed her a tissue.

"You do look gorgeous baby," Mama said as she wiped the tears from her eyes with the tissue I had given her. "It seems like just yesterday, as a frightened eighteen-year-old, I was bringing you home from the hospital. Now look at you. You're all grown up. I can't believe you're about to be a married woman." Mama wiped at her eyes. "I couldn't be more proud of you and all of your accomplishments thus far baby."

"Okay Avery, enough with all that," Auntie Mina said. "We need to get her into her dress. Time is slipping by fast. The wedding is at one thirty and it's already noon. We still have a ton of pictures to take and we need to make it over to the church at least fifteen minutes before the ceremony begins."

Auntie Mina was taking her wedding coordinator duties very seriously so from that moment on, everyone in Aunt Elsa's house was moving at the speed of light. With Auntie Mina's direction, we quickly flowed through all of the traditional pictures that brides take before the ceremony.

Cameras flashed as I posed with my grandparents, parents, aunts, uncles, and cousins. Before I knew it I was sitting in the back of the Duesenberg next to Daddy and headed to the church.

We arrived right on time and the parking lot was already packed. Where did all these cars come from? I didn't even know my parents knew this many people. Only a few of my friends were expected: Moni, Anya and her boyfriend, and Kirby had traveled to Baton Rouge from Atlanta. The rest of these cars had to belong to my parents' friends.

The Duesenberg circled the driveway and stopped in front of the doors of the church. One of the ushers knocked on the door to see if we were ready to exit.

Daddy motioned to him for him to give us just one more minute before he opened the car door. Daddy turned to me and said, "Kami darling you know I love you, right," Daddy asked. "Are you sure that this is what you want to do?" He touched my hair. "I know everything has been planned and a lot of money has been spent, but you mean more to me than any of that. If you feel uncomfortable in any way about this, you don't have to marry Christian today. We can go to the Camelot Club and have a big ole party instead."

I smiled and placed my hand on his cheek and said, "Yes Daddy I'm sure."

With that, my father kissed me on my forehead and smiled. "Let's go get married then," Daddy said. He tapped on the window and the usher opened the door.

Daddy got out of the car first and then reached back into the car to help me out.

My dress was kind of big so it was difficult to maneuver. Our first attempt had proven to be unsuccessful in that my shoe had somehow gotten tangled in my slip but eventually, after flashing everyone my new lace panties, Daddy, the ushers, and the driver were able to get me out of the car. "Alright, that show is finally over," Daddy remarked curtly as I smiled and shrugged my shoulders while being hoisted upright onto the sidewalk.

My mother and Auntie Mina gave me one more look over, adjusted my tiara, and moved into their positions in the precession.

The large wood doors of the church swung open to welcome the bridal party.

Before we centered ourselves between the large wooden doors I peeked inside the church.

Christian was rocking back and forth on the altar. He looked nervous as Hell.

Thank God Daddy was there because if he hadn't been, I'd have probably run. But even though I wanted to run, the thought of leaving Christian at the altar was too much to handle.

Daddy looked down at me.

I nodded.

It was our turn. As we centered ourselves between the two large wood doors that flanked the entrance to the church, we could hear a quiet gasp. Everyone was looking at us as Daddy and I made our way down the aisle to Luther Vandross's *Here and Now*.

Everything about the day was elegant and regal. From the dress, to the orchids and stargazer lilies that decorated the church and reception hall, to the open bar and custom menu our guests were dining on, everything was laid out to the nines.

Auntie Mina had simply out done herself by renting out the Camelot Club in downtown Baton Rouge, where membership was required to enter.

No expense was spared as we partied on the thirty-fifth floor of Baton Rouge's tallest building, overlooking the Mississippi River, dancing the night away.

DECEMBER 26, 2003

Bzzzzzzz. Bzzzzzzz. Bzzzzzzz.

Christian's cell phone vibrated loudly against the change in the pocket of his jeans. He had stepped out of them and left them in the middle of the floor when he got into bed around midnight.

I couldn't believe he was still sound asleep despite all the noise. I shoved Christian trying to wake him. He let out a loud grunt and continued with his sleep. The rattling change had awakened me and I couldn't settle back in. Who was calling him at three in the morning anyway?

I rolled out of bed and stumbled over to Christian's side of the bed in search of the phone to silence it. I wanted to go back to sleep. After searching each pocket of his jeans, I retrieved the phone from the very last pocket that I checked. Dominique Wilkins had called him several times back to back. Dominique Wilkins had been a star basketball player for the Atlanta Hawks for many years. I didn't know that Christian knew Dominique. He never mentioned that to me but who knows, maybe Dominique had bought a car from him. I silenced the phone and placed it on the bench at the foot of the bed.

No sooner than I settled back under the covers did the phone start buzzing again. I got up to turn the phone off again but by the time I made it back to the bench, the person hung up. Now I was getting irritated. I turned around to get back in the bed and then stopped. *Why would Dominique Wilkins be calling Christian at three in the morning?* My Spidey senses were now on ten.

I tiptoed back to the bench, grabbed Christian's phone, walked out into the formal living room, and took a seat on the sofa. This room really was beautiful.

The furniture had arrived on December twenty-third. I had been so busy with Christmas that I hadn't had a chance to truly take it all in. Looking at the living room was a way to stall the inevitable.

Nervously, I dialed the number back and, as expected, a woman answered. "Christian, I've been trying to get in touch with you for hours. The pipes busted at the house baby."

"What house? Who is this?"

The call disconnected. I dialed the number back several times with no answer. I had a bad feeling. I had to get to the bottom of this. Who was this woman and what house was she talking about?

Although boiling inside, I decided to play it cool and not mention anything to Christian. I only had a small window of time before Dominique reached out to Christian to tell him what happened. In an effort to delay that process, I took Christian's phone upstairs and hid it in Ethan's toy box. Ethan was notorious for playing with Christian's phone. He was always mimicking his father by walking around with his blocks up to his ear pretending to be on the phone just like Christian.

Hiding the phone in Ethan's toy box would buy me some time until I could get "Dominique Wilkins" back on the phone.

In the early am, I would take Ethan over to Lynie's with me before Christian rose. Lynie and I would call Dominique from there. Perhaps she would answer a number she didn't know and we could arrange a meeting before Christian even found his phone.

Content with my plan, I slid back into bed next to Christian and went over the details in my mind until I drifted off to sleep. I needed all of my energy for later today- the day of reckoning.

FEBRUARY 14, 1996

"Hey Mama. I need your help," I belted out as soon as she answered the phone.

"Oh lord child what have you gotten yourself into? What's wrong? Is everything ok?" Mama asked in a panic.

"Calm down Mama. Everything is fine. Actually great. Are you ok?"

"Chile, I was about to say, I got enough stuff going on with your sister over here. Daddy and I found some reefer in Dia's purse and she swears us up and down that it was really Oregano. I don't know what kind of fools she thinks we are."

"What? Not again. She keeps at that story because it worked on both you and Daddy the last time. You two had no clue what was going on until I told y'all to watch out for her. That's why she thinks y'all are fools."

"You stop that Kami." Mama scolded. "You're always thinking the worst of your baby sister."

"I don't think the worse of her. She is always in some shit."

"How is school going?" Mama asked changing the subject.

"Grad school is in full swing and it is kicking my butt."

She giggled. "I knew something had to be going on. We missed you and Christian at Sunday dinner."

"I know Mama. I'm sorry. I'm just trying to figure out how to stay afloat. I have an enormous amount of work due and have been consumed with trying to get myself acclimated to the rigor and expectations of this program, unfortunately to the detriment of excitement in my marriage. But, tonight is going to be different."

"Yea Kami, You're going to have to do something. It can't be all work and no play. You can't expect to keep a husband that way madam."

"Ugh, I know Mama, that's why I'm calling you. I can't allow our first Valentine's Day as husband and wife to be as uneventful as the first few months of our marriage. All week, Christian has been trying to get me to tell him what I wanted to do to celebrate. We are on a shoestring budget and just paid my tuition at Agnes Scott, which, by the way, cost us a fortune."

"Tell me about it. Private schools are no joke. We are still paying bills from your time at Spelman" Mama agreed.

"Christian always goes out of his way to surprise me, so I know that regardless of what I say, he is going to do something special."

"You do have a dilemma my dear, what are you going to do?"

"I was thinking that my gift to him could be to be a dress-up dinner at home but, I need some pointers. "I wanna make something special. You know, a romantic dinner."

"Ohhhh," Mama said teasingly, "Sounds like you two are about to start working on my grandbaby.

"Let's hope not. I have way too much going on with school right now."

"Umm hmm," Mama said with a chuckle.

"Anyway mother," I said blushing. "Any ideas on what I should make?"

When Mama and Daddy married, she like me couldn't cook very well, but over the years she had become an amazing chef. Neither of us had any excuse because my granny, her mom, could throw down. Now, Mama could make any creole dish from memory and dining at her table was like a little slice of heaven.

"Why don't you do a crawfish ettoufee? That ought to kick things off on a hot and spicy note."

"Now Mama, you know I'm an amateur."

"Yea, that recipe can be kind of complex, what about shrimp creole with potato salad?"

"Mama, I wouldn't dare attempt to make potato salad. You know you're the potato salad queen."

"No really honey, the shrimp creole and potato salad are both real easy. I can give you both of my recipes. I would offer to come over to help, but your Daddy is taking me to Panos's and Paul's this evening."

"Must be nice," I said. "Maybe one day soon I'll get to go back."

Mama continued, "So for the Shrimp Creole, the way I do it is, I chop all my seasonings first and get that out of the way. You need celery, garlic, onion, bell pepper, green onion and parsley. After that, you start your roux."

Mama quickly rattled off both recipes as I took copious notes.

"I think I got it," I said.

"Let me know how it turns out."

"I will. You and Dad have fun at dinner and I will talk to you later. Love you."

By the time I hung up the phone with Mama it was already noon. I grabbed my purse and darted out the door toward the grocery store. Since I didn't have a clue what I was doing or how long meal preparation would take, I had to get moving if I was going to pull all this off by the time Christian made it home from work.

Once I had dinner on the stove, it was time for me to get dressed. I looked in the mirror. *What happened to me?* I looked a mess. My hair was all over the place and I had sauce all over my clothes. I hopped in the shower and rinsed away the smell of the fabulous meal I had just prepared.

What was I was going to wear, I wondered. I decided on a red slip dress that hit my curves in all the right places, sans underwear, and pulled my hair back into a tight bun. Then I added a touch of blush to my cheeks and lip-gloss to my lips. Lastly, I slipped on a pair of sky-high patent leather pumps. I admired my reflection in the mirror. *Boy did I clean up nice.*

I didn't know whether Christian would be more excited about the meal of the fact that I didn't have on any underwear. I smiled impishly as I thought about how Christian was going to react. My thoughts were interrupted by the rattling of Christian's keys at the door.

I turned to the mirror and gave myself the "you go girl look" and then sauntered into the living room. Christian's jaw visibly dropped when I entered the room. He broke out into a huge grin handing me the dozen roses he had in his hand.

"Happy Valentine's Day baby," Christian said.

"Happy Valentine's day," I said.

"I see you have plans for us."

"I do. But first, why don't you go shower and change into the clothes I laid out for you on the bed."

While he showered and changed, I opened the champagne that had been chilling and poured two flutes full. Dammit. I forgot the bread in the oven. I rushed over and removed it just as the edges were beginning to char. Thank God it was salvageable. Everything was finally ready.

I surveyed the candle lit room. This was the first time we had used the Tiffany flutes we had been given as a wedding gift by Auntie Rose and the Wedgwood china Mama gave us. Everything was so elegant and delicate.

Just as I finished plating the shrimp creole and potato salad, Christian walked into the dining room. He looked so handsome in his black pin-striped suit, white shirt and red tie.

"I decided that maybe we could dress up for dinner at home," I said.

"Sounds like an amazing plan," Christian said with a smile on his face.

After dinner, Christian said, "I would like to propose a toast."

I raised my glass and Christian said, "To my amazing wife for making this the best Valentine's Day I have ever had and to our amazing union, may we love each other for the rest of our lives."

We tapped each other's glasses and tears came to my eyes. Taking Christian's hand I said, "I have another surprise for you.""

I slowly led his hand under my dress. When his finger reached my special place he gasped and then broke out into another huge grin.

"No panties... Nice," Christian said through his smile.

I got up and shifted Christian around in his chair to face me and then went straight for his belt and zipper. I slid his pants to the floor, then dropped to my knees and placed his manhood in my mouth and proceeded to stroke him up and down with my lips and tongue until I felt him throbbing inside of my mouth.

Christian moaned as I continued to suck and stroke until I took him right to the edge of release.

I pulled him out of my mouth and turned around so that my firm bottom was in his face and slowly bent all the way over and touched the ground.

My special place was directly in his face, open, waiting for him to take me from behind.

He stood up like a lion focused on his prey and thrust his manhood deep inside of me.

Maybe Mama was right, if we kept at it like this, she would get her grand baby sooner than we had planned.

With each thrust, my special place hugged and clung to him gripping and pulling him further inside sending chills throughout my body.

Neither of us could contain ourselves any longer, and finally, I released around him, creating his own special pool.

My wetness excited him to the point where he could no longer delay. He held me tighter and in one final thrust, he released inside of me causing our elixirs to mix and run down my legs. Our bodies went limp as we collapsed into each other's arms, sank to the floor, and dozed off into a deep peaceful sleep.

DECEMBER 27, 2003

I was determined to get a face-to-face meeting with Dominique, but to do that I needed to get her on the phone. She had stopped answering Christian's phone. Lynie had always been my ride or die and so I went to her for help. My plan was to use her phone to make contact.

It was amazing that I made it out of the house without Ethan waking Christian. His normal routine was to come into our room and wrestle with his dad. This morning, I turned his little behind around right at the door and ushered him back upstairs to get dressed. I had to bribe him with Chick fil a to get out of the house without making breakfast.

There was no time to waste. Every second I was not with or headed to meet Dominique meant giving Christian an opportunity to get to her and weasel his way out of this.

We hit Lynie's doorstep a little before seven. Ethan ran upstairs to see Big Colin and Little Colin. He always got really excited when we went to Auntie Lynie's house because he knew it would be a day full of fun and games. I knew he was going to be entertained so there was no need to worry about him listening to grown folk's conversations. He had grown nosey and was always trying to figure out what the adults were talking about. I guess that's something that comes with only children. They are around adults so much that it's hard for them to act like children sometimes.

With Ethan occupied, I caught Lynie up on the previous evening's events.

"What's going on girl," Lynie asked. "I heard the urgency in your voice this morning when you called."

"Oh Lynie." I wasn't sure how to begin. How do I tell her that Christian was cheating again? "Last night I got a phone call. Well not really me." I had to stop to catch my breath. "Christian's phone was ringing late last night. It woke me up, and I tried to ignore it but every time I thought it stopped ringing, it would start again. I couldn't take it any more so I got the phone out. Someone named Dominique Wilkins was calling. I thought oh my goodness, that's the basketball player." I could hear my voice catch.

Lynie was frowning.

"Christian has been doing business with some pretty big names in music and sports, so I didn't really think much more about it. I silenced the phone and went back to bed. And then Lynie, I thought to myself, why on earth would Dominique Wilkins be calling Christian at three in the morning?"

"I went out to the living room and called the number back and some woman answered. Lynie, Christian is up to something again. I've been through this with him too many times already. Just when I think we're on the right track, something else happens. I've forgiven him so many times I'm unable to forgive myself for letting him treat me this way. Each time it chips away a little more at my self-confidence and my soul."

Lynie sighed. "How can someone who claims to love you so much hurt you like that, Kami? How does he call that love?"

"Christian lies his way out of it every time. I know my only chance at the truth is talking with this Dominique."

Lynie leaned over, kissed my cheek and said, "You're my big sister. I'll do anything for you. But know that once we do this, once we go here, there is no turning back. Are you sure you really want to know what's going on? You can't hide anymore," Lynie asked.

"I'm sure," I said. "I want to confront her in person, and I need your help and your cell phone to do it." I need you to call Dominique's cell and help me set up a meeting with her. She won't answer calls from my phone any longer. Then I need you to roll with me to keep me calm. I'm really not sure how this is going to go down."

"I think we need to do all of this away from here. Let me get my jacket and let's go."

Lynie's husband Colin and Christian were extremely close and if Colin suspected that I knew what Christian was doing, he'd tell Christian.

So as not to tip him off as to what was going on, Lynie yelled, "Colin. Kami and I are going out to do a little shopping. Will you be ok with the boys for a little while?"

"Sure honey y'all go ahead. Have fun," Colin yelled downstairs.

As soon as we got into the car I said, "Lynie, dial Dominique's number from your cell because she may have spoken to Christian already and she might recognize my number."

I needed to meet her. I wanted to hear the truth from her lips, because I would never hear it from Christian.

Lynie dialed the number and Dominique picked up on the second ring. She looked over at me and handed me the phone.

"Hello Dominique," I said. "Please don't hang up. I am a woman dying inside and I desperately need some questions answered. I promise I won't scream and make trouble for you."

"I'm listening," she said, but her voice sounded shaky.

I knew I had to keep her on the phone until she agreed to meet with me. "Look, I've been through this with Christian before. You're not his first. But every time, he lies his way out. I don't blame you. You're as much a victim as I am," I said.

I heard a sigh on the other end of the phone. I quickly continued before she hung up. "Please just meet me for coffee to talk? It can be somewhere public. I promise I won't attack you or do anything crazy. I'm way past that point, I promise you. Please, just a few minutes of your time."

There was a pause, but she wasn't hanging up. I squeezed Lynie's hand and waited.

"I'll meet you," she said. "I'll be at the Starbucks on Roswell Road in forty-five minutes."

Then she hung up.

"Did you hear that," I asked Lynie.

"Yep. Starbucks here we come."

Lynie and I headed for the Starbucks clear back across town close to my house all the while filling the air with meaningless conversation. All I could think about was my marriage coming apart in tatters around me.

When we pulled into the parking lot, my heart was beating so fast I felt like it was about to pop out of my chest.

Lynie touched my arm and said, "Remember, stay calm. People go to jail for losing their tempers Kami. It's not this girl's fault. This is Christian's MO. He's been doing this to you since you two married. Let's get our questions answered and leave, okay, sissy?"

I smiled at her reassuringly. I was known to have an explosive temper so I really needed this reminder from Lynie. "I won't snap," I said. I thought about it for a second. "I think I really just want closure. I want her to say it out loud. I can't keep living like this with Christian. This life is turning me into someone I'm not proud of. I don't even know this person I've become. Do I care more about preserving my lifestyle than how I am being treated? I can't take his lies any longer. The deceit is eating away at me." I felt hot tears start to run down my cheeks and I flicked them away with my hand.

"You're right," Lynie said. "You need this if you want to get out of this cycle. It's not healthy."

"I just want clarity and peace," I said. "If we stay together, I'm going to hate Christian and for Ethan's sake, that can't happen."

We took a seat inside, close to the door, and waited on Dominique to arrive.

Twenty minutes passed, and I began to get antsy. "Where is she? I asked. "I think we need to call her again."

Lynie called Dominique's number several times with no answer.

Finally, we decided to try her from my phone, praying that Christian had not given it to her to block just yet.

She answered.

I put the phone on speaker so Lynie could listen in while I caught my breath. "Dominique, I'm here at Starbucks waiting on you. Are you still coming?"

"There's a change of plans," Dominique said. "I'm not meeting you today."

"But why?" I asked.

"I decided it's not a good idea."

My heart sunk to my stomach. Christian had gotten to her and she was obviously shaken up.

"He got to you," I said. "He told you not to meet me."

The silence on the phone was thick.

"Listen, you don't have to meet me. Just please tell me what is going on with you and my husband. If you don't tell me, I'll never know the truth. He'll just lie to me and lie to me until I believe him. I need closure and you're the only person who can give that to me."

Dominique paused a moment and asked, "What do want to know?"

"How long have you two been dating?"

"Well over a year. We met right after his father passed away."

That bastard. Here I was thinking things were all good between us and he started after another woman.

"The other night when you called and I answered the phone, you said something about the pipes in a house, what house were you talking about?"

Dominique paused for a moment and then said in a soft voice, "Christian and I have been living together or should I say, he got me a place about six months ago."

Six months ago, I thought back. "He got you a place at the same time he bought me the house." My eyes met Lynie's. She'd made the same conclusion.

"Did you know that Christian and I just moved into a new home not far from this Starbucks," I asked.

"Yes, I knew that."

"Dominique, you knew he was married. You knew he just moved into a new home with his wife and child. Why continue a relationship with him?"

"I love Christian and he loves me. He told me that things were not going well between the two of you and that you two were going to get a divorce."

I had heard that story before from Wynter.

There was silence, then she said, her voice a little louder and stern, "He knows you were messing around on him as well. We were going to just ride it out until one of you couldn't take it anymore."

"Lies. Dominique, he's telling you lies."

"I don't think so. When my son called the old house asking for batteries I just knew that would probably be the breaking point for the two of you. But you decided to stay. That confused Christian and me."

My blood was boiling. *Was he really trying to wait me out? What the hell?* This marriage could have been over long ago if he didn't want it. In fact, when you think about it, the marriage really was over long ago.

"Christian tried to play like your child was crazy and that you were someone he just helped out from time to time."

"No Kameleon, our relationship is a lot more than that. When Christian goes out of town on business, I am with him. Sometimes when he tells you that he's going out of town, we're really still here in Atlanta staying at a hotel in Alpharetta. We met in hotels for months before he rented me this house. He said that renting a house was far more cost-effective than continuing to get hotels every week. So, when Christian isn't at the house with you he's at the house with me. He's here every chance he can get."

I was trying to control my temper.

Lynie put her hand on my arm.

I could not believe that he had rented this bitch a place, bought furniture, and was playing fucking house. Here I was, thinking he was out of town working and instead he was at a hotel in Alpharetta fucking this bitch. *Ohhhh* weeeee. It was a good thing Dominique had decided not to meet me because at this point we would have probably been rolling around on the floor in Starbucks. She wasn't rude but, there was no respect for the fact that she was talking to Christian's wife. It was almost as if she had convinced herself that this was okay for some reason. Or, I thought, Christian had convinced her there was nothing to his marriage but a paper.

My life flashed before my eyes; from my first Mother's day, to being stalked by Wynter to now. Christian had not kept one single promise that he had ever made to me. He couldn't love me. How could he treat me like this if he did? I was nothing more than a trophy to him. I fit into his perfect little world. He couldn't care for me or take care of Ethan because he was always somewhere else. Come to think of it, he was never around. He bought me gifts to cover up for the fact that he was living foul.

Deep down, I knew she wasn't lying. All of the dots were connecting. No one could make this shit up. Only someone who was involved or had been a part of the situation could tell the story like this. Christian was living two lives.

"Listen, Kameleon, I am going to be late for work so I really have to go. I know it doesn't mean much and you probably won't believe me when I say I am really sorry you had to find out about Christian and I like this. No woman deserves this."

If only she knew the half of it. "Thank you for talking to me. I appreciate it."

As soon as I hung up with Dominique, Lynie and I jumped in the car and I dialed Christian's number.

"Hey honey, where are you?" I asked in the sweetest voice I could as I turned on to Roswell Road headed in the direction of my house.

"I got a late start today. That dog gone Ethan took my phone and put it in his toy box."

"That's just shameful," I replied, trying to hold my voice steady so as not to give away the rage I was feeling inside. "I told him to stop playing with your phone. What side of town are you on?"

"I'm actually at the Ford dealership right up the street from the house. Why, what's up babe?" Lynie and I were only two blocks away.

Who did this mofo think he was fooling? He knew damn well that I knew about Dominique and that he had put a halt to our face-to-face meeting. He was feeling me out to see what I was going to say.

"I'll be there in a minute," I said.

"Look Kami, I don't know what you're up to but I don't need you coming up here acting a fool. I have to do business with these people."

"Then I suggest you leave there quickly because I don't give a fuck about your business or those people. I said I am on my way." I hung up the phone and turned in the driveway of the Ford dealership just as Christian was trying to pull out. I blocked his path with my BMW and as he tried to go around me, I rolled down my window. "You better pull that motherfucker over or I'm going to drive straight through it," I screamed out the window.

Exasperated, Christian stopped the car and nervously got out. With his hands visibly shaking, he walked toward my car, I revved the engine and shot forward, barely missing him. I wanted to kill that motherfucker.

Lynie screamed and pulled up the parking break just as I shifted the car into reverse, trying to hit him again.

Christian hit the trunk of the car with both hands and yelled, "What the fuck are you trying to do?"

"Kill your ass," I shrieked. "I am sick to death of your shit."

I looked up at the dealership. A small crowd had begun to form on the showroom floor to witness the spectacle in the driveway. No one dared to come outside.

"I've stayed with your raggedy ass for eight years, constantly forgiving, turning the other cheek and you continue to put me through this bullshit. Who the fuck do you think I am? I don't deserve this from you Christian. I have given you everything. Everything I have and it's still not enough. First it's the bitch from Somalia, then its phone calls from children. Children, Christian. And now Dominique. This shit ends today."

"Kami, you have to stop," Lynie said. "Someone's going to call the police."

I slammed the car to a stop and got out, getting in his face. I jabbed him in the chest with my finger. "You know what Christian, you win. You finally win. I am done with your ass. Done with trying to make this marriage work. It's over. I'm getting a divorce." I turned around to get back into my car. I could see Lynie's frightened face in the doorframe. I turned back to Christian and said, "I recommend you not come home tonight because I tell you, someone is either moving out or dying and it's not going to be me. I already know you have somewhere else to stay so this shouldn't be a problem for you."

I gave him the finger with my left hand as I spun out the driveway headed toward home.

SEPTEMBER 28, 1996

"As each month passes it's getting harder and harder to move," I told Sherri as I awkwardly tried to adjust my weight while sitting under the hair dryer at the salon. "This is the largest I have ever been in my life. I'm so uncomfortable." I giggled.

"Guess Mama was right. This is what you get for being freaky with your husband on Valentine's Day," Sherri said. We both giggled. "When is your due date again?" Sherri asked sarcastically. She knew my due date. We had been teaching together for a while and had become best of friends. In fact, she was one of the first people I told when I found out I was expecting.

"Stop trying to be funny," I said with a slight grimace as I tried to adjust in the chair once again.

"I don't know if that baby is going to hold out until his November first delivery date," Sherri said.

"Oh my God, look. My tummy looks like it's going through some sort of metamorphosis." As I patted my stomach for her to look, Ethan rolled over inside of me. Sherri and I watched in amazement as my stomach physically took on various shapes. I was holding still, but it was moving in what seemed fifty different directions.

"It's like a scene out of a horror movie," Sherri giggled. "I can't wait to see him. He's an active little man already. Bet he's a handsome guy too. I'm already in love."

"Tonight there's supposed to be a total eclipse of the moon. It's so exciting. You know, they come around only once in a lifetime."

"Girl, you're talking about eclipses and I'm sitting here looking at your stomach do flips. You know the old folks say that eclipses cause unborn children to do strange things. Maybe that's why he's doing flips inside of you today." She patted my stomach. "You settle down in there."

"I'm not sure why he's jumping, but I agree. He needs to settle down."

By the time I got home from the salon it was already dusk and Christian had dinner ready. He only knew two recipes, one of which was something he called Seafood Newburg. The only issue I had with his Seafood Newburg was that it was made out of that imitation crab stuff and being from Louisiana, my Creole card would have been revoked if I was caught enjoying such a thing. I like real crab in recipes but, I was always happy when he made dinner for us. Hell, I'd have eaten a hot dog and beans if he was saving me work.

Instead of going straight inside to eat, I went to the bathroom to take my bath.

I came out all clean and my hair was pretty. I then sat down to eat the meal my husband had prepared for us. I felt good about my life.

After dinner I asked Christian, "Baby, take me outside."

I was way too big to even see my feet so I knew better than to try to wobble down the stairs that led to the garage alone.

Christian happily walked me outside. I'd been talking about this eclipse for the past week. He grabbed my arm and we walked out to the front yard.

It was a nice autumn evening. The sky was clear and the air was crisp and fresh. It was unusually cool for this time of year. Normally things in Atlanta didn't cool down until right around October but, tonight was unusually pleasant.

As we passed the back bumper of the car that was parked in the driveway, a gush of wetness came from between my legs.

"Oh my God Christian. I think Ethan is coming." I leaned back against the car and tried to look down at myself.

"What do you mean he's coming?"

"My water just broke."

"Are you sure? Maybe you're peeing on yourself."

"Of course I'm not peeing on myself fool. I know what's going on."

So much for the eclipse. We were in complete and total panic. Ethan was not due for another six weeks.

Christian rushed me back inside the house and helped me change into dry underwear. He then ran around from room to room gathering things for my go bag while I called the labor line and our parents to tell them we were headed to the hospital.

Dr. Moore met me at the labor center.

"Our plan is to try to stop Ethan from birthing," my doctor said. "He's six weeks early and I am concerned his lungs may not have had a chance to develop properly."

A nurse came up to get me into a wheel chair and rushed me into the emergency room.

Dr. Moore gave me a shot in the attempt to try to slow Ethan down.

After the shot they moved me into a beautiful birthing room and the wait began. Christian and I had been at the hospital for two hours by the time our family arrived.

We were all in the room having a good ole time watching the Best of Richard Pryor when the nurse walked in and threw everybody out of the room. She needed to check my cervix to see whether the shot they had given me had slowed the process.

"The first shot doesn't seem to be working," she said. "I am going to send Dr. Moore back in," she said as she exited the room.

Dr. Moore came in shortly afterward. "Kami, we're going to try one more time," he said. "As you already know, our goal is to try to keep Ethan inside for as long as possible. This time we're adding a steroid shot for Ethan just in case this second shot doesn't work. The steroid shot is going to help mature his lungs so he won't have to be on a breathing machine when he is finally born."

After fifteen hours of trying to slow Ethan down, the doctor finally decided it was best to just let him come on. I was finally given my epidural.

Now, I'm deathly afraid of needles, but after all the pain, waiting and worrying, I gratefully took that shot. The labor had grown unbearable.

"Oh, Christian," I would cry out and he'd come and mop the sweat off my forehead with a cool cloth. Or, my mom would rub my shoulders. The last half hour was the worst.

After twenty-seven and a half hours, I delivered a beautifully perfect baby boy.

As I held my son for the first time, I studied his tiny features. He was the most incredible sight I had ever seen; so red, and he had a tiny little cleft in his chin like his Papa Louis. I could not believe Christian and I had created this and I had brought this amazing being into the world. I wondered what kind of man he would be when he grew up, and I quietly thanked God for this blessing while quietly repenting my decision about the other two children that could have been. I had finally done it. I was finally a mommy and I was absolutely fine with it.

JANUARY 10, 2004

The last time I'd seen Christian was when I tried to kill him at the Ford dealership. Now I was happy I wasn't successful. Crimes of passion are real. I see how they happen. I was out of my mind that day, and so humiliated and hurt from all Christian had done. The last few weeks allowed me to think about how life could be without Christian.

Ethan was struggling with the separation and wondering why Daddy didn't spend the night with us anymore.

Moni, who was my attorney, had completed the separation agreement. It had been done for a week or so, but I wanted to really think it, and everything else, through before I shared it with Christian.

With him out of the house, I had the space and time I needed to think.

Every apology and lie he told me just pushed me further and further away from him. Further away from the life I knew and further into an unhealthy space. I had been his conscious. Now he was going have to find his own.

The garage door opened and Christian walked in. He was picking up his last few items and was going to look over the separation agreement.

"When you leave today, I'm gonna need you to leave that garage clicker and your key. You have no right to just walk into my house. You do not live here anymore.'

"Our house you mean? I still pay all of the bills in here," Christian responded.

"No, I meant exactly what I said. My house. And, since you couldn't seem to remain faithful in our marriage, your past actions serve as excellent leverage to ensure you will continue to pay the bills in here."

"Look Kami, I didn't come here to fight with you."

I moved aside to let him enter the kitchen and I watched as he looked around the house and took a seat at the kitchen table. You could see in his tired eyes that even with all he had done, he still considered this *home*. Thank goodness Ethan was with his Nana because we would never have gotten anything accomplished.

"Listen Christian, I don't want to make this process long and drawn out. Please don't make this harder for me than it already is. I hate that things have come to this with us. I don't want to hate you and at the rate we're going, I will. We have a kid to raise, so we always need to be able to be cordial with each other."

After a long silence Christian responded in a sad tone, "I can't believe that you're actually done."

"Every time you cheated, with every apology, I've fallen deeper and deeper into the abyss and further away from us, from our marriage. Further away from our beginning. I don't even recognize myself anymore and I damn sure don't recognize you. Who are we becoming? What are we waiting on? Who are we kidding?

Christian placed his elbows on the vast wooden table and cupped his head with his hands staring down at the wood.

I continued, "This relationship has been over for a long time. I can't do this with you any longer. Before we go over this separation agreement, is there anything that you want to share with me? Why were you so dishonest with me all these years? Why didn't you say something to me if you were unhappy in our relationship?"

Christian looked up, his hands were still on his head and he had a single errant tear that had escaped out of his left eye.

"How do you tell the person you love the most what you're doing?" Christian asked. "I didn't want to see you hurt Kami, but at the same time I couldn't stop."

"Christian, it has to stop. Somebody is going to get hurt. Here's the separation agreement that Moni drew up. I had her to include all of the things that we discussed. "We will share joint custody of our son and make decisions together."

Christian had agreed to $4,000 a month in order to support the household and Evan's tuition.

But today, he looked at the custodial agreement and frowned.

"Is there anything that I'm leaving out?"

"No, babe, I think that's about it," Christian said. "I hate that I'm losing time with Ethan. I hate that we've come to this point. I'm so sorry Kami. I never meant to hurt you. I hope one day you'll find a way to be friends with me and that we can raise our son together."

"Maybe with time and distance that can happen but for now, I have one request. If you agree with everything in the separation agreement can you please not show up to the hearing?"

"You don't want me there?" Christian asked questioningly with his brows furrowed. His eyes were searching mine looking for any sign of weakness and any indication that perhaps I didn't want to go through with this.

There was a long pause.

"I just think that it will make things more difficult for both of us if you're there," I eventually replied.

"Ok Kami. If that's what you want, I can do that," Christian finally said.

FEBRUARY 20, 2004

A beautiful Monarch butterfly danced passed. I stood on the top step of the courthouse taking in the movements of the exotic creature, contemplating its journey and considering its connections to mine. The weight of my cocoon had been lifted and I had earned my wings. I could breathe again. The life I had lived for so long was no longer.

I walked to my car, inhaling deeply the scent of the fresh rain that had passed through and was now evaporating. For the first time in my life, I felt free.

I had surrendered and I was grateful.

I was grateful to Christian for not contesting the divorce and for staying out of court.

I was grateful for my new life and the opportunity to live it on my own terms, flaws and all.

I was grateful for the quiet and calm in my mind and in my heart.

As I drove home, I thought about how peaceful I was in this moment and quietly whispered, "God, please allow this peace to be still within me."